THE RUBY CRADLE

THE GEMSTONE SERIES
BOOK TWO

JAMES L HILL

Published By RockHill Publishing LLC
PO Box 62241 Virginia Beach, VA 23466-2241
www.rockhillpublishing.com

Time is the lie
An illusion of what's done
Is done
Future a ghostly image
The false view of perfection
To come
Life the deepest well
Heart and head eternally swimming
In darkness
When old becomes new
The soul's consumed by fire's
Joyous pain
No escaping the present
Dreams are memories that haunt
Us now

CHAPTER I

CRIMEAN WAR

Aberash, dressed in white, climbed over the piles of bodies, pulling those who clung to life to the buckboard wagons. A fog of blackness from the anguish, fear, and horror of each person's death invaded her mind. Growing thicker with each death until her sight was near blindness as she performed her duties on the battlefield. Other women, whose white dresses, like hers, were nearly dyed red, searched for the living among the dead. The brave and valiant, whose courage could not be measured in how long they endured the fighting, or by counting the number of dead lying among them, now forgotten and abandoned as their armies marched on. And be they Russian or Ottoman, they were heaped upon the wooden planks of the wagons and taken to a church in the square for treatment.

"Work quickly, my sister," commanded Aberash, "we must save all we can before the night falls."

"There are so many lying in the fields," Abagail lamented, "he shall have more than his fill of souls this night."

Mind your words, sister, they betray your nature. We work side by side with women here. But you are right, we cannot save all these men from Deyhezas. He will grow ever more powerful with each battle fought, and bodies he consumes. However, he gains the most from those he takes alive, so let's deny him all that we can. Use your powers to quickly find those with even a glimmer of life left in them. It is better they die in our company than here in the wasteland.

The wagons thumped and bumped as the women pulled them over the fallen and delivered another dozen to the already over-flowing makeshift hospital. The church held meager supplies of bandages and wooden splints. The women, some maidens and some older, stitched and sewed the men's wounds. Those Ottomans who could walk joined the line of wounded heading to Balaclava. The Russians headed for Sevastopol, which had already fallen. A Cossack captain caught the attention of Aberash.

"Captain, where is your commander? I need to have words with him."

The captain laughed through the pain and lifted his mangled arm. His sword locked in his grip, unable to release it, frozen there by the length of time held and the wounds received. Pointing towards the window, he said, "You can speak all the words you want, but I'm sure they will do no good. His body was blown apart before my eyes by a cannon ball that struck mere feet from me. Luckily, I was thrown from my horse and only broke this arm. I was able to continue my fight into the city and to this glorious victory."

"Name the general who commands this regiment. I will speak with him."

"Careful, nurse," warned the young captain as he looked around the room. "Asking questions of this nature could get you hanged as a spy."

"I seek no military information. I want to know where I might find medicine and bandages for your men," cajoled Aberash.

"You waste your time here, sweet lady. Those that would die here will die, and those that live will die later. But if it makes you feel better, straighten my arm and pull the shot from my leg, and if I am alive come morning, I will take you to my General."

S moke from cannon fire caused the morning sun to shine dimly over the battlefield. The moans of the dying quietened to a faint hum. Bodies lay half-buried in pools of blood-drenched mud. White plumes rose slowly from the field and death drifted on the whispering wind, a smell of burnt flesh and gunpowder. Man and horse disemboweled and scattered over miles was testimony to the madness that had claimed this land. Men too old for battle took to the field scavenging the dead for their worldly possessions. Stripping them of boots, clothes, and coins, then heaping their bodies together and setting them alight.

Shuza had fallen but at a great cost to Tsar Nicholas Pavlovich. The siege lasted three gory days. Each sunrise a gate flung open and screaming scimitar-waving troops flooded the battlefield as arrows rained down. The Sultan's knights with razor-sharp crescent-headed spears rode out knowing they charged into Firdaws, never to return to the safety of the walled city.

The Cossacks were swift and outmaneuvered the cannon batteries that defended Shuza. They rode fast and hard from the Black Sea drawing fire on one flank, cannon balls falling short of their ranks. But cannons still caused them to ride through a rain-storm of rocks and debris ejected from the earth by iron balls, stripping more than a few from their horses as effectively as a line of riflemen. The cannon-ball screams heralding death to all who approached. They rode a line of certain death that kept the thunder of hooves and iron balls in constant flow like a tide upon the shore. Neither could cease for fear of death washing over their position. This was the plan of the Cossacks, to draw fire, to invite death, to play a devilish game with the Ottomans until it was too late for them to change position.

A second wave attacked from the north, crossing the Alma River under cover of night. The Ottoman soldiers held the city for most of the day, repelling infantry and cavalry charges. Although most of the fighting was in the fields surrounding the city, the heaviest losses on both sides came late in the afternoon when brass guns formed a line to the east of the city. They were smaller, lighter cannons, pulled into place by soldiers. They loaded and fired five-pound balls, not as devastating as the big twelve- and twenty-pound iron balls, but effective. Multiple cannons fired at the same target, then repositioned slightly below and fired another round. The bombardment collapsed the old walls of Shuza and finally the Cossacks charged in. Swords and bayonets turned the streets slick with blood. No retreat was sounded. No surrender offered. The fighting went on until the last man gave his all.

Night drew near and fear rose within Aberash. The black cloud, the specter of doom filled her thoughts. A growing panic, something new to her overtook her being. *Abby, where are you?*

I am in the fields with the women. We have found hundreds of men still alive.

You must get out of there now. He is coming!

Mother, I am fine.

Aberash had thought she was well past spawning. Her straight black hair had turned bleached white and now straw-like. The last decades had hardened her once soft creamy skin. And having mated with men for centuries, she knew that another maiden was beyond her, then came Abagail. She kept her by her side at all times, even in this dangerous environment she felt she needed her Abby under her watchful eye. She had lost daughters to the dragons before; it was a pain she could not bear again.

Abby was a little over a hundred years old, she appeared as a sweet little redheaded child but spoke and acted as a woman much older. Maybe that was why the other nurses followed her. They were running back and forth with the most injured men and bandaging those who could be quickly set on their feet again.

The horizon was set ablaze by the departing sun. The darkness was coming soon, and she had never faced a dragon.

I can feel him. This battle is of Deyhezas' making, he will come to claim his prize, and none he prizes more than us. I can't lose you. We must get to the Black Sea now, only the water can protect us.

S creams grew louder and filled with terror, flashes of flames were seen from the city walls while a dark figure moved through the field, and the men tried to convince themselves it was battle fatigue. The fires… the result of the countrymen burning the dead to guard against disease. A horror, greater than what any man had faced on the battlefield gripped the hearts and minds of the survivors that night. The brief flickers revealed death, gruesome and wretched, finishing the deeds of men.

Deyhezas was no apparition brought on by the ravishes of war. He was real flesh and blood drawn to the pain and suffering of war. In the darkness, he sniffed out the living among the dead and slowly ate them bite by tasty bite. He savored the anguish even more than the blood he rolled in and licked from his claws.

He inhaled the chilling cries and exhaled flames from his

snout. Burning both the living and the dead. He reared up, flapping wings that were as long as his body. Great mounds of muscles on his back between three rows of spike vertebrae powered the massive, scaled wings. He was a blur in the smoke-filled sky to the city dwellers for a moment before crashing down again. Deyhezas wallowed in the fields like a pig in slop but stayed away from the city. His horrid roars struck fear throughout the night, but as boastful as he was, he still feared men. He rather feasted on the injured than face the meager number of armed soldiers on the walls. His strength was but a fraction of what it once was, and he knew capture was a real possibility. Especially if Aberash was nearby.

Deyhezas could sense an inkling of her presence. She had been here. Perhaps, even taken part in the battle. But she could also have others with her, hiding themselves from him. The air held a faint scent of the fishy women, as distinct and desirable as the fear of men in the city, which could be a trap, and he wanted no part of it. The dragon contented himself with a feast of thousands slaughtered for him. How easy it was to push Tsar Nicholas to war.

Men dreamed simple, and were easily manipulated by goals of land and power. Their shortness of years made them eager to grab at the smallest of triumphs. This had always been their weakness, and he used it to his greatest advantage.

For centuries, he and his brothers laid in wait for their return to the world. Aberash, the Fool, had brought them back. Now her folly would feed them for an eternity. The world of men had grown too numerous to count. And the sea witches' numbers had dwindled over the ages. This would be the age of the dragons. This time they would rule the world with flames, and all would suffer.

Aberash and Abigail returned to Shuza at first light. The devastation of the battle was unimaginable. The ghoulish repast of the night was sickening to all who ventured from the city. Bodies towered and burned, just enough to be recognizable as the soldiers who gave their lives for some unknown cause.

Crimea was a small insignificant country on the Black Sea. A steppingstone for Nicholas on his drive to topple the already weakened Ottoman Empire. He sent his troops on the pretense of freeing the Holy Lands once again.

Aberash, Abigail, and the captain made their way north through the battlefield on an open buckboard wagon. The two women driving the single horse drawn wagon, the captain in the back on a stretcher moaning from the rough ride. His right arm had two splints, one above the elbow and one below, to set it where it was broken. It was then wrapped tightly against his chest to keep it immobile. The bullet had been pulled from his left leg with steel forceps. Abigail slit the wound another two inches to expose the vein it kicked. Using a thin line of sheep intestine, she carefully stitched it and sewed the wound shut, instead of cauterizing with a red-hot iron as was the usual treatment. He was securely cocooned to the stretcher with bandages for the long miles to the sea. The stretcher was tied to the wagon sides by four short ropes that allowed it to swing a bit to make his journey more bearable. The wagon rocked and bumped as its wheels sank into shelled craters and climbed over charred bodies. Every few feet the wagon would drop sharply as a pile of crisp remains piled three or four high crackled and gave way.

This is not how we left these poor souls. Abigail had tears streaming down her face. Never had she seen such a sight.

This was his doing. He left them here like this for us to see. He torments me every moment. Letting me know this was my doing. Confessed Aberash.

No, you cannot blame yourself. You had no way of knowing the evil they would unleash.

Oh, but I did. Why should I think eight hundred years or a thousand in darkness would change their hearts?

"Aggh. If this accursed ride doesn't kill me then the smell definitely will," complained Prince Alexander Menshikov, the wounded captain.

"Abby, go back and tie the captain's stretcher tight," said Aberash. "We are nearing the end of the battlefield; we will go to a fast trot."

A snap of the reigns and the white stallion skipped into a faster pace. He too wanted to be free of the smell of death that surrounded them. The buckboard tossed wildly as it crossed the last mounds of desolation. Abigail wrapped one arm around the side railing of the wagon for stability and placed her left hand on the chest of the young prince captain. Her touch soothed and quietened the man.

His eyes fluttered and stared up at her in a warm gaze. She was but a child, not quite marrying age, but he loved her. Her amber eyes set fire to his heart. Her tender slick pink lips spoke of mysteries she should not have knowledge of, yet for the taking, there they were. Her crimson tresses set his mind aflame with desires.

Careful, Abby, this man is not at all well.

I know, Mother, but he suffers so much. I will just ease his pain a little while we make haste to the sea. He may not survive the journey otherwise.

The three were taken aboard the Russian schooner Nikolai II, the flagship of Admiral Vasily Zavoyko. The admiral recognized the prince instantly and ordered his medical staff to take him below. He welcomed the two women into his stateroom for tea and supper. Fresh meat and fruits were laid upon the table, and the admiral was as gracious as he would have been to Queen Victoria. Even though he had no idea who they were or why they were on his ship.

"I thank you for taking such good care of the Prince. I am to believe he performed exceptionally well in battle… judging from his wounds, of course."

"I'm sure he performed his duties with honor and distinction," Aberash replied politely.

"Ah, his safe return comes with a price," the admiral's face hardened slightly as he locked eyes with Aberash.

Her eyes, dark, slanted and deeply set, held comforting

wisdom that beckoned the Admiral's attention. She was a mature woman, yet not scarred with the wrinkles of time. A commanding figure but also in distress. "Not a price," Aberash said softly, "a humble request. Withdraw your troops from the peninsula. Negotiate an amical treaty with Sultan Abdulmecid I."

The admiral looked far off into the distance as if he were pondering the possibility. Then his bright blue eyes turned as black as an onyx. His face twisted and his teeth bared. A voice, not his own, spoke from afar. "Did you think it would be as simple as this, Sea Witch? Merely cast your charms upon this simple man and be done with me. NO! I shall reign a thousand years and a thousand more after your death."

"What can you hope to gain from this carnage? Have not enough suffered at your will? I did not free you to reap such havoc on mankind."

"FREED ME. Imprisoned me and my brothers you did." The admiral stood transfixed as the words poured from his mouth. Expressionless and devoid of thought but a passion in his words that were commanded from another. "And this havoc you accuse me of is man's own doing. I was content with sword and spear, but I awoke to a new scent on the wind. The black powder and sounds of shot… that is what it is called… yes, I like this very much. Mankind has thrived in my absence, why should I not take advantage of progress."

"This be not progress!" screamed Aberash. "You will cast humanity back a thousand years. Back to the Dark Ages with this madness."

A knock on the door broke the admiral's trance, "Yes. Enter."

"Begging the Admiral's pardon," announced the ship's chief surgeon with a queer look on his face, "but the Prince requests the company of Florence Nightingale."

"Who?" All three asked in unisons.

"Well, he said the girl who sings like the nightingales of Florence. I am assuming he's speaking of the maiden."

Mind what you say and do aboard this ship.

Worry not for me, Mother. I will be on my guard. I fear for you, though, I sense the pain growing inside you. Don't be taken in by his words.

bigail went below to the captain. His words were a mixture of gibberish and slurred lewd advances. The doctors informed the girl the Prince had a large dose of a new form of opium called heroin to alleviate his pain. They were amazed at how clean his wounds were and the precision of the setting of his arm. She left little for them to do except deal with the pain the best they could. "His arm should heal completely," the doctor commented.

She told them how to sew together arteries and veins to stop the loss of blood. Better ways to immobilize their patients to help with the healing process. And most importantly, boil their instruments before and after each use. She spoke with such authority they thought she was born a doctor. They thanked the young girl whose name would spread as Florence Nightingale.

The prince healed and returned to lead a regiment of fifteen hundred infantry, Cossacks, and gunnery brigades. Prince Alexander learned a lot at Shuza, especially that fixed cannons were useless. He commissioned iron guns mounted on wagons drawn by a team of horses. The large cannons fired twelve or twenty-pound balls for assaults on fortified positions. The lighter brass cannons with their own wagon wheels could be maneuvered easily by a three-man gunnery crew. The cannoneers, as he called his three men gunners, loaded and fired a five-pound bag of shot. He deployed these forces against the enemy's mounted troops and infantry, with great effectiveness. Clouds of lead spread before the charging troops killing and wounding many of them. A fine mist of blood rose in the ranks of the enemy. His cannoneers shredded the Sultan's lines and battle plans.

Alexander's advances in the Crimea came to a stalemate when Britain, France, and Sardinia allied with the Sultan. Thousands more troops flooded the war zone. The fighting was fierce. The blood flowed like a raging river across the land. Abigail, by orders of the prince, was not to be harmed. The combatants recognized the tents with the red crosses as safe zones on the battlefield. Florence Nightingale and her nurses were seen racing across the battlefield to ferry away the wounded. The Turkish medical forces, demarked by the red crescent, were given the same courtesies on the battlefield. Although these women in white were not targeted, many fell as a bullet knows no friend.

Prince Alexander captured the guns of the Turks at Balaclava and was preparing to retreat with his bounty. The British commander, Lord Cardigan, gave orders to his lieutenant to send the Light Brigade after the Prince's retreat.

The assault needs to include all the valley.

The lieutenant ordered the mounted troops to make a frontal attack against a heavy artillery battery across the valley. The horses poured down into the valley led by the Lieutenant. Six hundred men with swords drawn followed. It was pure suicide, and all knew it, but no one refused the order.

Clouds of black smoke spread over the valley. A gathering storm of annihilation formed before all eyes. Cannon balls whistled through the air and crashed down on the British forces. Thunder rang like church bells in the valley calling the doomed souls to judgement. Chunks of metal and rock ripped flesh from horses and their riders. But they never stopped. None turned back, they continued the charge with feverish obedience. They rode towards an unattainable victory ignoring undeniable defeat. A few made it across what was to become known as The Valley of Death. Badly outnumbered at ride's end they were captured or killed.

This is your doing, Deyhezas. When will enough be enough?

This is not by my command, Sea Witch, although I do enjoy the sight. I thank my brother, Vargrerot, for this feast of humanity.

Her Majesty is young and easily fooled by her military. We shall feed well this night, brothers.

The slaughter of the British Light Brigade only convinced the Queen she needed to commit more troops to the Crimean War. The French increased their efforts in support. Ships crossed the Black Sea from the Sea of Marmara. Their guns pounded the port cities around the Black Sea and troops marched into Russia.

The Russian navy was put to the test as Admiral Zavoyko tried to run a blockade of Tagarog. Three steam-powered frigates and the Nikolai sailed into the center of the British and French lines. Aberash was aboard the English ship, The Victory. She had been tracking the Tsar for months and had finally found him aboard the admiral's flagship. She knows this is her chance, her only chance to bring the war to an end. They must capture Nicholas and force him to sign a treaty.

Do not engage the frigates. Give them a wide berth. She commands Admiral James, and he obeys. The frigates' guns light up the night sea and their flashes give away the Nikolai's position. *Aim high at her black sails. We must disable her and cut her off from the escorts. Once she falls behind, we must board her at all cost.*

The battle was as costly as any that was fought on land. The frigates' steam-powered paddlewheels allowed them to advance and fall back to protect the Nikolai. The sea was ablaze as ships both steamed and sailed were on fire near the Russian port. Twice, marines tried to board the Nikolai. First a French vessel rammed her, and her men repelled the crew with riffle fire and bayonets by forming a double line along her gunwale. Then the English destroyed her three masts leaving her dead in the water. But instead of abandoning ship, the Russian sailors took to the sword. Steel lightning flashed throughout the night. Clashing of swords mixed with screams of pain. Blood rain soaked the wooden decks. The English sailors finally set fire to the ship and left without the Tsar.

As the sun rose most of the British-French fleet had sunk. The three Russian frigates did no better and were going down slowly. Their massive boilers kept them partially afloat until they blew apart. Aberash abandoned the steam-powered frigate, The Victory, when a cannonball crashed through the boiler room spreading fiery hot coals across her bowels. She ended up on a French sloop with no sail.

The sea was littered with sailors. All floating and mixed together. Very few longboats had survived the fight and were fishing men from the water and bringing them to shore. Nicholas was not among them, neither the living, nor the dead. Aberash saw the dragon clearly in the flames swop in and carry him off. Deyhezas did not rescue the Tsar. He made sure Aberash would not get her peace treaty.

Tsar Nicholas I was found several days later, dead in a small village not far from Tagarog. His body was broken in many places, laying among the granite tombstones in a courtyard of a local church. It was obvious to Aberash and Abby the dragon simply dropped him to his death. Officially, it was reported he died at home in his bed, a victim of the weather and the sickness it caused.

You failed again, Sea Witch. This wretched piece of flesh was sailing to make a peace offering. Had you not attacked… Well, I will leave you to ponder that fate.

Aberash returned to the Black Sea, the weight of Deyhezas words clinging to her like the smell of rotting flesh. This war was not being fought neither for power nor control, not by the humans nor by the dragons. This war, like so many in the past decades, was being fought for nothing more than an ideology. It was a war that could never be won. Men weren't trying to win; they wanted to prove themselves right. Their way of thinking was better than the other's. Their form of governance was the only right way to live.

The dragons weren't looking for victory either. They were unleashing men's most vile and evil nature against themselves. Aberash felt that maybe the dragons were right. Perhaps, men had come to this of their own accord. Sure, they had a hand in pushing them into war, but they didn't have to push very hard. These dark thoughts drove out the light from Aberash's eyes. They dragged her down into the cold emptiness of the Black Sea. She lost all hope of ending this war. Perhaps, unwittingly or not, she knew when she returned the dragons to this world, the disease that plagued mankind would be eradicated in the only way it could, by the all-consuming light of the dragon's fire.

If this was to be the fate of the world, she wished to be no part of it. She sank deep into the darkness. Away from the voices of dragons, away from the battle cries of men, even away from the songs of her sisters. She sank down into the dark of nothingness and out of this world.

CHAPTER 2

CASTLES ARE ALIVE

With the death of Nicholas, the war came to an end in February 1856. Deyhezas had unwittingly done what Aberash failed to do. It was Nicholas who was the greatest threat and without him the alliances fell apart. Territorial lines were redrawn and places on the maps renamed. Unlike other wars of the past where there were clear victors and vanquished enemies, the Crimean War's only true victory was the joining of the Italian states by King Victor Emmanuel II of Sardinia and turning them into the country of Italy.

The vanquished enemy were the Ottomans, as much of its empire was gone and the nation of Turkey born. However, the Ottoman Empire was already in decline as much of its territories were seeking their independence. Many in the Ottoman world believed her allies were never engaged in maintaining her sovereignty, just in stopping the Russian advance further south. The Christians were equally content to see her fall.

France returned to her borders but left behind troops of the Foreign Legions to protect her newly acquired territories in Crimea. Although France got little out of the war, it recognized the need for modernizing its army. Horses and swords were being replaced by trenches and riflemen. Napoleon III had reason to worry about his post-war European neighbors, the war showed that borders were less respected by those with sufficient numbers and the artillery to back them up. He knew that stationary embattlements were a delaying tactic, the cannons now fired explosive shells shaped like bullets which had a better range and accuracy, but still the castles and their walls would slow the advance of an invading army. The way to win a war was to mount an offensive at the border.

Napoleon feared Germany was just such a country. The castles along the Rhine bristled with energy. Germany was building factories along her river and turning out steam engines in great numbers. The Germans were heavily involved in a new mode of transportation, the locomotor. She was putting down rails across the country that could move thousands of men to her borders in days instead of weeks. The iron horse, as it was called, could pull tons of equipment and armament. Crimea had shown a new way to move troops and supplies to the battlefield and it turned the tides of war. Wars of the future would take greater numbers of troops. Artillery would cut down soldiers at a distance never seen before. Germany was also developing larger guns that could only be carried by rail cars to destroy inland targets the way the naval guns crushed coastal cities.

England solidified her global power as Queen Victoria commissioned more iron battleships powered by steam. Her navy spread from the far reaches of the East, Hong Kong and India, where she was known as The Empress of India, to the Americas with her holdings in the Caribbean. She had learned from the past. The Spanish Armada, which failed, and her country's own failure to hold onto its colonies in America, all hinged on her nation's naval abilities.

Queen Victoria felt the Evil spreading across the continent. The death of Nicholas was just the beginning. Or maybe just another step in the growing malady of nations. Her own family had suffered from similar tragedies. Did she not gain the throne after the death of her uncles and father? A dark cloud was rising from the castles across Europe, casting a familiar shadow on the land. The sound of steel being fashioned into weapons was the music of this latter half of the nineteenth century.

The British Isles were protected by sea and ocean, but were not impenetrable. A new naval fleet was needed to protect their shores. Steam had done away with sails. Not dependent on the wind and its direction made the ships more formattable. But the large paddlewheels, either at their side or in the rear, were a weakness that needed to be addressed.

The battles in the Black Sea were won or lost when cannonballs destroyed the ships' paddles. One shot could crash through multiple paddles, reducing their effectiveness to power the ship. Or a well-placed one could disengage the wheel altogether. The wheels had become the only means of propulsion on some battleships. Mobility and maneuverability were the strategies for naval warfare. Gone were the days of sailing lines of warships passing each other with cannons blazing. Fewer, but more powerful guns were being employed and their accuracy meant ships needed to avoid direct contact with their adversaries. One shot completely disabled a ship and took it out of the battle.

The Queen got what she needed in a new system, the underwater propeller or prop. Placing the propulsion system under the body of the ship further protected it from cannon fire. Two independently controlled propellers also aided in the ship's maneuverability. Iron, steam, and underwater props were turning the Queen's navy into a dominant force.

J eremy took a position in the Royal Court as the Duke of Hampshire. Shera's powers helped him to convince those who knew the family of the former Duke that Jeremy had gone to Norfolk in the States. He had returned home to Portsmouth to oversee the building of the new Royal Navy.

Jeremy had left England decades ago as a young man in the navy. Seeking fortune and to make a name for himself in the colonies, he had not been back since. All was changed by a run-in with a storm and an evil queen. The storm sunk his ship and with it his fortune. The queen turned his name to piracy as both the hero and villain of the American Revolution. But defeating her did not return him to normalcy, he had spent so much time away from the world, all he desired was to spend his remaining days in isolation with Shera. But they could not escape what Rhema's curse had begun. She altered their being and the very world they lived in, her thirst for revenge, starting the world on this path into darkness. For decades she had pitted one nation against another in hopes of destroying their navies.

The dragons used this air of animosity and furthered the push of their armies. Shera and Jeremy had felt the steady rise in power of the dragons. The outbreak of war on the Crimean

Peninsula sounded a death knoll around the world. Jeremy knew he had to answer it.

"She is ready. She needs to know what is coming," Jeremy told his wife.

"I know she will lead the maidens, but there has to be another way," Shera's heart was heavy and her eyes darkened.

"You know there isn't," argued Jeremy but with sympathy for his fearful wife, "Aberash is gone. Abigail doesn't know if she was killed in battle or is in hiding. You said her mind was slipping away. The constant haranguing was eating away at her. We need someone who can teach Zabella. Someone who can train her in your ancient ways. There is no one else."

Shera pleaded, "Rehema is pure evil! and lives in darkness. You, most of all, know the pain she can cause. She tortured us both, but you spent years in a grave because of her vile power. We cannot trust her, not with Zabella's life."

"She is the last person in this world I would trust," Jeremy agreed, smiling weakly. He spoke softly trying to hide his true feelings of the situation. He worked hard to maintain eye contact and the smile that felt so much like a lie. "I have no doubt that her contempt for us has only grown deeper with the passing years. And yes! She broke my neck when I was hanged as a pirate. I spent years living in the darkness of the grave when she beheaded me. Your mother enslaved you on the Emerald Lady and forced you to use your abilities against those you loved. She spread death for reasons only known in her demented mind. There is not one decent or good thread within her soul, but these dragons are far worse. I believe, nay, I know Rehema hates them more than she does us. More than she does mankind. She must know that in time they will come for her too. She was as much their jailor as Aberash. It is in her self-interest to see them defeated."

Shera knew Jeremy was right. Zabella would soon be Queen. The dragons were amassing armies around the world. They had grown powerful in exile. Their control over the hearts and minds of men was unshakeable. How else could one order so many into a suicide attack. And they had grown wise over their centuries of captivity. They would not confront the maidens or their forces in open warfare. They used their surrogates.

She felt Vargrerot's influence over the British monarchy. He was behind the death of Prince Edward, the Duke of Kent and Alexandria, Victoria's father. He had driven George the Third, mad, which was one of the reasons the colonies broke with the crown. Vargrerot, Shera believed, killed George IV's daughter, leading to his death shortly thereafter. Then William IV's reign was beset with riots and upheavals, no doubt more of Vargrerot's handy work. William's death left the throne to Victoria. And now she was building a mighty navy. Shera wasn't sure if it was an answer to the growing threat surrounding the Queen, or in response to her master's call.

The skies over Europe were thick with black clouds. Smokestacks pumped rancid arid gases into the air. The people were herded into cities to support the growing industries. They lived in crowded dirty slums. Suffered illness and hunger that swept through the population. Even with the entire family working, they earned little more than enough to keep them alive. Bleak was their outlook. Their existence was only to serve the expanding mechanized warlords. And their invisible masters, the dragons.

Jeremy and Shera knew the dragons had in some fashion banded together. They suspected that the dragons communicated while in their ruby cradles. They festered like a disease. In their exile, hatred for maiden and men was universal. It also left them starved for flesh, a hunger that was maddening, and only surpassed by their thirst for blood. There were wars in the Far East. Kingdoms in South America were falling to European invaders. They felt the claws of the dragons ripping apart the world of men.

Shera wanted Zabella to at least reach her fourth century before taking over. But she knew they didn't have the luxury of time. The dragons had driven Aberash from the world and now stood ready to unleash Hell upon mankind. The maidens were still too few to fight them on their own. Zabella would have to enlist the aid of men, a great many, to combat them.

Shera had learned much from Aberash and her powers had intensified since her ordeal, but she could not train Zabella. Her birth had been special. She was a strange being, born into both worlds and belonging totally to neither. Zabella could change to maiden form and live under water, but she could also survive there in her human form. The same was true of living on land, she survived without the need to return to the sea in any prede-termined time. She lived as a little girl for years on land. She aged slowly, unlike maidens who quickly grew to the equivalent of a young lady, then aging slowed to a crawl.

Zabella spent her baby years in the sea with Shera. She grew and matured as maidens did, but at age five her growth stopped, and she began changing into human form. Still breathing water but no longer swimming or behaving like a mermaid. Clearly, she desired to live upon the land. Her mind was sharp, and she struck out in anger against her sisters. Dark rage flooded the minds of those around her. And the other maidens found they were unable to block her tantrums or to soothe her mind.

Shera brought her to the surface world to live. First, on Usea, the maiden's home, but that failed to satisfy Zabella. Jeremy surmised she needed contact with other humans. He was right, she could feel the thoughts of humans and needed their company as she had needed the mermaids. As a child, she was unable to comprehend the difference between the two races. Why could she not have them both, and why did she need them. Jeremy knew what she desired; to run, to jump, to tumble, to play with children. Shera could not understand. The maidens could not understand, how could they? They only changed forms; they were still mermaid in or out of water.

"Zabella is both and neither completely," Jeremy held his wife tightly as they lay in bed. Although she had returned to his bed nightly, she left Zabella in the care of her sisters since maidens her age could not transform, and he felt the anxiety within her. "At first, I thought she was all of you, but I could not shake the feeling deep in my soul that she was part of me too. She is akin to a toddler who just learned to walk. She doesn't want to be held back. She knows there are others like her, and she needs them. We will move to the mainland for a while, she will be happy, you will see."

Zabella's growth slowed down considerably on land. She was stronger and more developed for a child her age. Her mind sharper, able to grasp ideas and concepts that other human children could not, but her body, her height and weight lagged behind. She remained five years old for years. But because of the disparity between her physical appearance and her mental acuities most people thought her an oddity.

Shera explained the situation to Jeremy, "Zabella can reach into the minds of those around her. She naturally learns the complexities of the world by absorbing what those around her know. I know what my sisters know and they of me, you know what I know because we share the link, it was forced upon you. For Zabella, there is no difference between the minds of maidens and those of humans. Soon she will be able to push her thoughts to humans as she does to her sisters. I think they will find it quite disturbing."

Shera and Jeremy took her back to the sea when questions arose about her age, only reappearing when those who knew them passed away or the family moved to another place. She lived with her maiden sisters for years at a time. In the sea she experienced growth spurts, doubling in size within a year, catching up to mermaids her age quickly. It seemed she needed both worlds to survive. Mentally, she was far superior to her sisters, the difference between human thinking and maiden was so profound that learning to master both made her greater than either. She could penetrate the maiden's minds without their knowledge and block them from her without effort. Many maidens feared her.

S hera had taken on an older form since the birth of her daughter. She appeared twice as old as her four-hundred-year-old sisters. She had deep lines on her face and her hair lacked the sheen of one her age. She wore it in a short single braided ponytail, with a swing of her head, the hair would twist itself down the middle of her back. It no longer ran to her upper thighs; it stopped halfway, just past her shoulder blades. It had darkened from vibrant green to matted black. She too could exist out of the sea for extended periods of time, although not for as long as her daughter. Jeremy didn't mind the change. She still was as amazing in his eyes, just as the day they met.

He felt the residual effect of his life with Shera as a benefit. Sure, he aged quickly into a fifty-year-old man, but then his aging slowed to a turtle's pace. If asked he would say, "Rehema's curse was my blessing. I would have been dead a long time now, instead we share an amazing life, My Love."

"Perhaps. But my mother's intent was not to make you happy," Shera reminded him. "She still has much malice in her heart towards you and all mankind. I can feel it. Even a half a world away, not a sun rises or sets without her distain for the world of men."

"Surely, a hundred and twenty-eight years has softened her a little."

"I wouldn't set foot on that island," she smiled but the color drained from her face as she pictured her mother. "And you wouldn't last a minute there either. Even stripped of her powers, she is still a force. I am sure there are a million horrid secrets that she holds that no loss of powers could rend from her. Are you sure we should do this?"

"Who else but Rehema can reach our daughter's mind? You tried."

"It is sometimes open and welcoming, but then it can be black and twisted. We maidens lose our way, so I don't know if even my mother can reach her. A shared consciousness is a difficult thing to manage. Zabella may come back damaged beyond repair. Rehema may take advantage of the situation to commit some unspeakable act of vengeance on her."

"She's her grandma, all grandmas love their grandchildren," Jeremy tried to joke, "even the ones who hate their children."

Z abella, Abigail, and six maidens made the journey to Rehema's Island. It was shrouded in perpetual clouds. They were greeted by fifty maidens who now lived on the island tending to the ex-queen. They remained loyal to Rehema, believing the curse on Jeremy and Shera was justified. The war, not her fault, and her exile that resulted was the true crime. They informed the group Rehema never came down the mountain.

She lives alone in a cave deep in the jungle. No one ever sees her. We used to take fish to her, but we ceased decades ago as the offerings would rot untouched. She eats only fruits and nuts that grow on the mountain. Her mind, thoughts, are hidden from us. SHE SEES NO ONE.

I am here to see her.

Send her up! The rest may leave.

Abigail looked concerned. *We are not to leave her alone. We will all have an audience with you. Or no one will.*

I will see the abomination and only THE ABOMINATION!

Zabella assured her escorts that she would be alright and began the trek through the jungle. The rest remained at the beach. The jungle was hot and steamy. Zabella didn't see any creatures on her way up the mountain. It was obvious all life had abandoned the island when Rehema took up residence. It was deathly silent except for the sound of a constant wind. The wind blew strong, and in every direction, away from the island. No ship would ever sail to the island. It existed in a hurricane storm. The island was hidden, and barren, save the trees and bushes which were stunted in their growth. Rehema was sucking the life out of the island.

It was dark before Zabella reached the top of the mountain. She walked the small path to the mouth of the cave; it was like she had been here before. From the cave opening Zabella could not see the beach. See could not see the ocean. She could not see anything through the thick white clouds. Rehema lived in total isolation.

Come in, abomination.

Why do you call me that? It doesn't hurt my feelings.

I do not care about your feelings.

Zabella went to her knees and crawled through the opening. The cave opened to a single spacious area. There was room for many things inside, a bed, chairs and tables, chests, but there was nothing. The cave was a void in solid rock. Rehema sat near the back in the blackness.

Not what you expected, is it?

I did not know what to expect. No one speaks your name. No one carries thoughts of you. Only my mother and father bring you to mind now and again. Those thoughts are never kind or pleasant.

No, I suppose they wouldn't be. So, Aberash is dead, is she not?

We do not know. No one can reach her.

Good! Serves her right. I warned her not to release the dragons.

Zabella remained close to the entrance. She was ready to run. She was not scared, well, a little, but she had been warned. Her mother said do not trust her. Her father insisted she keep her guard up at all times. Rehema's violent nature could turn on her. "She was trying to help my mother and father."

They didn't need help. They were uncomfortable, I'll grant you that, but they were in no danger. A few hundred years and I would have released them from their prisons. Aberash freed the dragons to steal my throne. And look what it got her! Rehema laughed loudly; the sound echoed. *I am glad Aberash is dead. No. No, not dead, lying in some dark hole tormented by the demons she conjured up.*

Zabella could hear no more of Rehema's venomous rant. She loved Aberash. She spent years with her and Abby in the Mediterranean listening to stories of their golden age. She was the first to open her mind to the powers within. Taught her to use the strength of the stones, powers of the sea, energies of the sun. Aberash was a great healer, helping others while she was slowly torn apart. Zabella began to crawl out.

Where are you going? Your mother, that ungrateful... she sent you here for my help. Come. Sit. You have much to learn. I will speak no more of your beloved Aberash. But your mother was not innocent. She defied her queen and consorted with a man. Her sins caused the death of an innocent creature and for that I punished her. It is important that you know the whole truth. You see, man is not worth saving. Love is a weakness. Your mother and father now know how cold true love is and the fire of desire leads only to death.

"My mother was right to exile you. But only you have the

knowledge we need now." Zabella crossed the cave and sat inches away from her grandmother. Still, she was invisible to her, only the amber glow of her eyes gave proof that she was truly there in the darkness. Zabella could neither hear nor feel her draw breath. Her body gave no warmth to the surrounding air. Rehema was dead to this world. "My father said speaking with you will be like sipping poison, over time you taint everyone. So, tell me what I need to know to defeat the dragons. And only what I need to know."

Your father sent you? That is surprising. I would have thought him dead by now. You see, not all things I did turned out bad. But I can't tell you what you need to know, I will have to show you, or more accurately, take you where you'll see for yourself what you are fighting.

Rehema studied the girl. She knew the girl was not much more than a hundred years old, but she seemed much older. She was tall and lanky, probably not losing much height in her transformation from maiden to woman. Her thick black hair framed her dark face and blackish eyes, curling at her shoulders. She had a serious countenance that demanded respect, and still, an innocent that spoke of trust and love. Her mind was strong. Rehema tried a couple of times to invade her, to slip into her subconscious while she spoke, but found no crack she could exploit. Zabella had a power that even she was unaware of, a will of iron and fortitude beyond her years. Her spirit shone like a beacon in the darkness. It drew others to her and brought out the best in their nature. A quality that took the other maidens centuries to develop. Zabella impressed her.

Zabella had not been able to sense her grandmother, other than the thoughts she imparted to her. She wondered how she had aged in the century as a human. Zabella wondered if the darkness hid her shame or some deformity. She knew Rehema would not reveal anything she did not want to show her. In these years, she blocked herself from the world of the maidens, but it was obvious she knew all about what was going on beyond this island. Perhaps, syphoning information from her entourage at the beach, or maybe her power was so strong she could exist in the mermaid world without them being aware of her presence.

Jeremy warned his daughter that Rehema would want something for her help. What that would be, no one could tell. Maybe her freedom, maybe her throne, but she had no power to grant anything. If she was to help her, Zabella would need to convince her to do it for the sake of humanity and the good of the world. She now knew those two things had no sway over the ex-queen. They had changed her physically, locked her in human form. Removed her from the world, but they could not alter her spirit. She was full of contempt, hatred, and darkness. It was hard for Zabella to determine if Rehema blended into her surroundings or did it emanate from her.

W hen Zabella left her home in Portsmouth, her father was working on the new propeller system. He didn't talk much about his work and she didn't intrude on his thoughts, but she felt that progress was a bad thing. He was a man of sheets and sails, not steam and underwater paddles. He wasn't so against the creation or use of the machines; he was opposed to what they were being built for. The propellers and steam engines made sailing much faster, goods could be delivered across the oceans in half the time. However, he wasn't building cargo ships. He was building battleships. Although he didn't like it, he knew they would soon be needed. Unless his daughter could do the impossible, the world was marching steadily toward war.

CHAPTER 3

THE FALL OF THE EMPIRE

Rehema's eyes grew brighter. They became as bright as the sun. The cave illuminated with an eerie glow. However, there was an absence of shape and shadow. Her eyes lit up the darkness in Zabella's mind. She could see the deep green of forest and bright sunshine. The grass was long and soft beneath her feet. It waved and swirled around her as she walked across the fertile fields. Zabella ears filled with the sounds of birds, insects, and small woodland creatures. The wind moved her effortlessly across the countryside. The air smelt sweet and familiar as if she knew this place.

Rehema had taken control of her mind. Two icy hands gripped her at the temples and frozen her. Her body was no longer her own. The power of her grandmother was irresistible. Icicles grew and drilled into her mind, sapping her will as they did.

She was weightless. Her vision became distorted as if she was looking at the world through a sheet of ice. It was not a world she recognized; it was not of her time. She had experience couplings with Aberash, learned through her experiences, but that was sharing. This was an invasion. She struggled to keep the freezing cold that spread through her muscles from taking control, her breathing became harder, her heartbeat slowed.

Stop resisting. You want to learn of the dragons; I will teach you.

A jaundice haze slowly replaced the pale blue world. It grew hotter. *KEEP YOUR PROMISE, DRAGON QUEEN!* Flames of crimson, orange, and brilliant yellow raced from her, consuming everything. Thousands of voices crying out in pain, calling to her, "Rehema, why?"

Rehema's eyes, fiery and cold, surveyed the misery. A vast faceless army marched into the flames before it went white hot. In the black center, a place devoid of life, a sound of wings beating, drumming up a storm, a hurricane that striped away time. Zabella tried to make sense of the images, but the blackness overtook her. The curtain was dropped, and emptiness followed.

Oh no, those thoughts are not for you. That is not a path you need to travel. Your concerns are much further away.

Reality was coming to a halt as she was moving through space and time. She had never felt anything like what was happening to her in the cave. Zabella labored to maintain her identity as the years peeled away. This was nothing like what she experienced with Aberash where their minds coexisted. Her thoughts mingled with Aberash's and she could see another life as if looking through a window. This was very different. She was losing her memories. New ones flooded in. Her thoughts were being replaced by another's. Not Rehema's, someone older. A memory of a memory from a memory. She transcended lives.

Zabella saw her reflection as she rose to the surface of an inland lake. The sun above caused a mirroring effect on the water which broke away in ripples as she emerged. The last vestige of herself rolled away on the waves and was gone. Her long blonde hair draped to her waist, she grabbed it, squeezed the water out and wrapped it in a twist around her head. She pinned it on top with a sharp silver spike from her waistband.

The white linen tunic clung to her as she walked along the shore-line. Every curve was outlined in fine detail. Her legs had fully formed but she was still unsteady on her feet. Regaining her balance was always difficult for Appolonia as her transformation left her three feet shorter on land. In her natural form she was eight and a half feet from nose to tail. Walking in the water gave her strength and reassurance. Slowly her balance returned to her, and she was once more graceful in her stride.

Apollonia started up the road towards Sardo, a small fishing village in the Roman province. She always chose the lake as her entry point to avoid detection. It was fed by a deep subterranean river that connected it to the sea. She was well-known in Sardo as a senator's wife, which kept anyone from questioning her comings and goings. And her husband was seldom in the tiny hamlet, always much busier with the provincial affairs back in Rome. Like many senators of the day, he kept a palatial estate far away from the chaotic capital, a haven for his family. He was on his third wife, and his sons and daughters had moved on to lives of their own. His current family consisted only of a wife he rarely saw. She soon reached the place where her Centurions should be waiting. They were there but no longer awaiting her arrival. The dozen soldiers had been killed.

From the bloody scene, she knew they fought hard and long. The company of soldiers had slain three times their numbers before dying. The earth was scorched. Her guards were ambushed not by soldiers alone, but a dragon as well. He had obviously hoped to find her with the men.

She placed a hand to each man, friend and foe, seeking knowledge of who had attacked them. But they all had passed from this life and took the information with them. Apollonia sniffed the air and tasted the blackened earth from her fingertips to pick up the scent of her nemesis. Although strong, her senses could not identify the dragon that laid waste to her guards. She would go on to Sardo where she feared the worst for its people.

The Roman Empire was in turmoil. Attacks like the one at Sardo were happening more frequently. The outer provinces had fallen decades ago, and the armies had retreated to Rome and places south. The northern provinces had been reclaimed by their people and they now marched against Rome. Not as a single force, but many separate waves of attacks by all her conquered people. Each seeking to take their measure of revenge. The once mighty empire was in its death throes. As great and powerful as Rome had been, its demise would be equally long, painful, and spectacular. Sardo was among the last of the northern territories Rome still controlled. She posted a full garrison there and another few miles to the south, less than a half day's march. Sardo was the first line of defense for the empire. Well-armed and fortified it was meant to repel or at least exact a costly toll on any invaders attempting to get past her.

Apollonia walked among the battered people of the city. Many were dead. The buildings crushed and burnt. From the beautiful, marbled villas and palatial estates on the surrounding hills to wooden-plank two-level slums of the city centers, everything that would have identified this place as a city was in ruins. Most of the dead were in the colosseum, as they naturally flocked there for protection. It was the only structure that was at least partially standing. One side of the great circular structure had completely collapsed. The other half had two or three tiers ripped away. Columns and massive stone blocks littered the colosseum floor. As did the dead. She made eye contact with one woman clutching her dead child to her breast.

It started at sunrise. The hoards came on horse and foot. The centurions sounded the alarms and fortified the gates. But there were so many. Too many, they scaled the walls in several places and the North Gate fell. We ran to the Colosseum and the remaining troops took up positions at the gates. Soldiers and gladiators fought side by side and kept the marauders out. At noon, when we thought they had turned the hoard away, we saw the black cloud circling. Then the lightning and fire. We were terrified, no, horrified, it was Jupiter himself that came to punish us. Who else could it have been? He chose the form of the beast. Devoured men, women, and children. Burned all that was around. I survived because the arena collapsed on top of me from His great weight.

Apollonia heard many such accounts from the survivors' minds she entered. From one soldier about to pass into the realm of the dead she heard, "Shabodun."

Another soldier lent her his eyes. Shabodun had dark brown wings and a matching stripe down his back. He had green leathery skin which blended into the trees around the town. His coloring must have allowed him to get close to her guards. His fire was limited, and he used it in short bursts to force the soldiers into small tight packs. Then he set upon them with claws and teeth. He was a young dragon, less than a hundred years old, which was why Apollonia was unfamiliar with his scent. She would not forget it now. He was like other young dragons she encountered. His skin had not yet formed the armored plating from centuries of absorbing the sun's rays. Or blackened to the color of midnight, much more efficient for gathering energy. His fire was quickly expelled, most times without any real control, so he relied on his claws and teeth to do his killing. His hide was susceptible to the soldiers' weapons, but the great mass of muscle under it gave him little to fear from men.

There had been a rise in young dragons over the last fifty years. The elder dragons had grown tired of battle and created and sent this new breed forth in their place. They were reckless and destructive, killing for pleasure as well as food. They did not try to remain unseen; they relished in the terror they invoked. Young and reckless, they felt themselves invincible.

Shabodun had left his imprint on the survivors of Sardo. Apollonia learned a lot from them before they succumbed to the terror. His own troops, which laid wounded from the battle, provided clear insight into his intentions. He had attacked Sardo because she was known to live there. He wanted her dead before he moved south to Rome. Wanted to make sure she would not interfere with his plans to topple Rome and Vargrerot.

Apollonia held no love or loyalty for Vargrerot. Shabodun and his army could take the dragon if he so desired, but she did not plan to stand by and let him destroy towns and cities along the way. Several dragons had plans to overthrow Vargrerot, all of them called for the lives of mankind. And when she could, Apollonia stopped them with iron chains, spikes, and the aid of men and maiden. The young dragons learned that they could not be killed but neither were they invincible. It took many men and maidens to defeat a dragon, but it could be done. Shabodun was not a very large dragon, he was still developing, the size of a large bull elephant, maybe two, he would be easy enough to shackle.

Vargrerot had grown old. He ruled the Roman Empire throughout its rise. He toppled the Great Egyptian Pharaohs, killing a dragon whose name was long lost in history. Now it seemed to be his turn. Shabodun was a lower tier dragon, sent to do another's dirty work. Killing Vargrerot would increase his power substantially, but his transformer would still be more powerful than he.

Shabodun knew that taking a maiden would amplify his powers greatly. He wanted Apollonia's life force to assure his victory in Rome. So, he hunted for her in the towns and cities as he marched his troops towards Rome. *Where are you, young witch? I smell your scent everywhere; taste your essence in every human I devour. Come to me and I will make your ending quick and quite pleasant.*

Why do you waste your time looking for me, when you know where to find me? Come to Rome and face Vargrerot. I'll be there waiting for you too.

Do not put your faith in that old cretin. He cannot help you. I will have his heart and his power.

Ah, I find that hard to believe. A young pup like yourself is a little challenge to Vargrerot. But I'm not here for his aid, quite the contrary, I will see you both fall. Two less dragons in this world are better than just one. If you want it, you can have his heart. Provided you are strong enough. And I will have the head of the winner.

Apollonia rallied the legions of Rome. She sent three to the hills outside the city to wait for the dragon to show himself. She had taken on the personae of Marcus Maximus, a general and head advisor to the Emperor Nepos. While she led his armies, Vargrerot controlled his plans. She could feel his presence on him, and she goaded Vargrerot to take to the battle-field personally.

Vargrerot, you must sense your reign is at its end. Time has caught up with you. It is what happens, but fear not! If you want your beloved Rome to survive you must come from the shadows and show your people your greatness. They have forgotten you!

Months of battles between the Romans and Germanic tribes were going nowhere. So many spears were broken, and so little wood was left to replace the lances, the soldiers took to using the spearheads as long knives to augment their swords. Thousands lay dead outside the city. Hundreds more fell within the city walls as attacks were launched and beaten back. Vargrerot would order a legion to charge the enemy lines and battle for days until all lay dead. Shabodun's plans were no better, night attacks or at first light, his troops would advance and take a few streets before becoming surrounded and in time slaughtered. Each encounter lasted hours, only coming to an end when no more reinforcements were sent to replace the fallen.

Apollonia tired of the endless conflict. The battles would not end until the dragons met. They both would welcome her death in the outcome.

Vargrerot, are you truly the coward I think you are? Will you let your empire fall to the hands of men, or will you step to the field of blood and protect what is yours?

Shabodun, where are you? I thought you had a thirst for maiden blood. We be three in this field, but you remain in the shadows. If you so hunger for my life and that of my sisters, come and battle for it. I am sure I will claim your heart before Vargrerot can consume it.

The dragons took the bait. On a foggy morning Vargrerot led his emperor and troops from the eastern gates of Rome. His massive body covered as much ground as two legions of his troops. One hundred and twelve feet of bony scales rippled through the mist. The Germanic tribes were afraid but stood fast before the advancing foe. They feared their own master and the death he promised more than falling before the monster.

Vargrerot reared up on his hind legs, towering over the battlefield. He let out a mighty roar of white heat. The blast spread outward as a giant ball of flame. All the Germans on the field cowered on hands and knees hoping to not be consumed as it rolled towards them.

A loud wind thundered across the plains, turning back the flames. The wooden shield walls of the archers and catapults toppled over onto the Roman troops, tossing them into bonfires of men and debris. Shabodun had landed to do battle.

Where are you, Apollonia? I hunger for your flesh and blood. I will claim her soul this day, Shabodun, and your heart. Your master, Deyhezas, put too much confidence in your abilities. With or without the maidens' blood you are no equal to me.

Shabodun answered with a fiery blast of his own. He swept across the field with his flaming tongue lapping up the front lines of Vargrerot's forces before the elder dragon leaped into his path. Vargrerot glowed a deep dark red and smoke rose from his back before he shook it off. His body swelled and he twisted slowly enjoying the feeling of Shabodun's fire.

Aaahhh! That does feel good. Loosens up the muscles. I haven't felt this good in a century or more. I thank you for that. But let me show you how a true dragon does battle.

Vargrerot leaped forward landing his front claws on the neck and back of Shabodun, pinning his head to the ground. He had fooled the young dragon into releasing too much energy too quickly. While he had him trapped, Vargrerot swung his twenty-foot tail sweeping away hordes of Shabo-dun's men.

Shabodun used his tail to sweep the old dragon off his feet, then he rolled over, crushing more of his men before taking to the air with a couple of flaps from his wings. Shabodun was less than a third of his opponent's size, but he was much quicker and more agile. Vargrerot rolled back and forth, killing more of the young dragon's troops. He was toying with the young dragon. *Are you really going to abandon your slaves so soon? No matter, I am not after them right now. I will feast on them once I'm done picking your bones.*

Vargrerot leaped into the air and with a single flap of his wings was upon Shabodun. He bit into his tail causing the young dragon to twist and turn trying to free himself, finally, he tumbled back to the ground. The two dragons squared off. Circling around each other stomping on men from both sides as the armies clashed beneath their feet.

Should we attack now, sister! The dragons are too busy with each other to ward off an attack from us.

Patience my little Azarin. They are still too powerful to take on now. Be ready with shackles and chains.

Azarin sat on her horse watching and awaiting her mother's signal to attack. The dragons were making a bloody mess of the site. The claws and teeth of Vargrerot opening huge gashes in Shabodun unfortified hide. Shabodun was holding off the more powerful Vargrerot. He used his quickness to get to the older dragon's back. The sound of a wing snapping made Azarin giddy.

Stay focused! When we attack, they will both turn on us. See how they withhold their flame, not wanting to infuse their enemy with power. They will not hold anything back against us. Be not fooled. We will face the full fury of their energy, and Vargrerot has much stored in that ancient carcass.

Vargrerot tried to escape the grip of Shabodun by flying. The young dragon held tight to the right wing, dug his claws into Vargrerot's side and was lifted high into the air. Vargrerot turned over and let himself crash to the ground on top of Shabodun. Vargrerot's weight broke bones in the young dragon's chest. He responded by clawing away at the broken wing until it hung by only flaps of skin and strands of muscle. With only one wing for Vargrerot, and Shabodun rolling on the ground in agony, Apollonia gave the order to attack.

Now, my sisters, before either can kill the other and absorb his opponent's power. Azarin, take control of Vargrerot's troops and turn them towards Shabodun. Azura, you do the same with Shabodun's men. We must keep the dragons engaged and confused until we can get our men in place.

The soldiers turned from the battle with each other and in response to the nonverbal commands attacked the dragons in whole. Their spears and swords sent pain rippling through Shabodun's skin making him aware that he still had not developed the scales he needed. Killing Vargrerot and eating his heart would transform his leathery hide to the thick plating he desired. The soldiers' attack infuriated him and intensified his battle with the older dragon.

To Vargrerot the assault of the soldiers was slightly noticeable, a swarm of flies to an elephant. He swatted the troops away with his tail while his teeth and claws fully engaged Shabodun. Snapping and swiping at the smaller opponent, opening much deeper wounds than did the swords and spears.

Apollonia, Azarin, and her other sister Azura who was enchanting to gaze upon with eyes of summer blue skies and hair to match, were far behind the men spiriting them forward. The men believed Azura to be a goddess and followed her commands blindly. The Romans charged down the mountainside and towards the melee. Massive iron chains and shackles were piled on carts and drawn by the humongous horses. The horses wore heavy metal plates to cover their breasts and sides. Leather and metal masks protected their heads. Their hooves pounded the ground like the beating of a thousand drums. The legionaries ran in front of the war horses to use their scutum shields to protect the bindings. Their scuta were specially built for fighting the dragons by covering the curved rectangular wood with brass plating instead of leather. They were heavier than the usual shields of the Roman legions, but it gave the men a measure of protection against the flames which they knew would soon be coming.

Vargrerot was the first to become aware of the mermaids' attack. Off balance and stumbling from the pain he tried to let out a powerful blast of energy. The fireball was weak but effective, the flames spread around the first lines and dropped many in the lines behind them. The rest resumed their charge as they left their knees. He was about to unleash another one when Shabodun jumped on his back. He clawed, bit, and did so much damage to Vargrerot's wing he withdrew from the battle.

The Maidens are both our enemies. We can continue this later.

I care not for them. First, I will have your heart, then I'll take care of the sea witches.

Anger fueled another blast from Vargrerot, immensely more powerful than the last, and stopped the mermaids' attacking force. He then pounded the younger dragon with his tail, curling it into a scythe and swinging it side to side, beating him in the face. Shabodun fell from his back into the dirt and Vargrerot hammered down his head even harder. He scurried off, leaving him to the Roman soldiers.

Shabodun bleeding, dizzy, and blind in one eye leaped into the air. His powerful legs pushed him high over the soldiers' heads and out of reach of their spears. He flapped his wings, causing dirt and rocks to be hurled in all directions. Then he rose from the battlefield. He circled once but thought better of attacking the Romans who were forming defensive positions and readying for battle. His chest hurt and he could not bring enough power to his breath to project a fireball. One powerful sweep of his wings carried him high into the clouds and he was gone.

Shabodun fought off the pain as he flapped his wings and rode the winds in the skies.

Apollonia would have to deal with him at a later date. She lost the opportunity to capture and confine either dragon, but she was elated that the Roman Empire had fallen. She felt it was a matter of time before she trapped Vargrerot who was severely wounded in the battle. His reign was over.

The remaining Germanic tribes charged into the city. Free of any influence from the dragons they ransacked the city. Killing and raping at will. Burning and looting the houses as they moved unchallenged by the soldiers. Misery rose from the once great city as she sank in a pool of blood. This went on for days as everyone was caught up in the frenzy of anarchy. Germans and Romans alike reveled in the freedom that came with the collapse of society. The time had come when those who could wield a weapon effectively could do as he or she wished. Slaves extracted their revenge from their masters. Centuries of Roman rule overturned. Those in power were made to atone for their sins and the sins of their forefathers.

Apollonia and her sisters had no wish to be a part of any of the battle's aftermath. They departed Rome as soon as the dragons had fled. She remained on task and began tracking Vargrerot through the countryside. His wounds made it impossible for him to fly, but as dragons go, he was as fast as anything on four legs. Apollonia, Azarin, and Azura stripped the warhorses of their armor and rode day and night following the scent of the dragon. His blood and anger left a trail that was easy to follow. They each pulled a wagon load of chains and spikes to capture him. They felt just the three of them could shackle the injured dragon.

The sun helped Vargrerot to heal. He was heading towards the mountains north of Rome where he kept a lair. More than sunlight, he kept others in this lair that would cure his wounds. Once he was more than a day ahead of the maidens he stopped in the foothills. He bit into his dangling right wing and with a horrifying cry ripped it from his body. A burst of flame from his mouth stopped the green oozing out his back. It was only at that time that he realized his left wing had been broken in several places as well. Knowing having one wing was as good as having none, Vargrerot's powerful jaws and massive teeth snapped off the appendage with a crack that resonated from the mountains. Followed by a howl that sent people running for shelter for miles.

Apollonia heard the dragon's wailing throughout the night. The bright burst of flames showed how enraged he was. The night glowed orange for hours. The mountain erupted and shook from his anger. He was several days away now, and they needed to return to the ocean as their maidens' powers were starting to wane. She wished she could have taken him, perhaps wounded, even killed him. She knew it would be centuries before Vargrerot would make his presence known again in this world. Vargrerot would wallow in his shame and defeat and plot his vengeance on the maidens and dragons. This was the plight of the dragons. They knew no comrades; they held no loyalty.

CHAPTER 4

OGRES AND WITCHES

A wall of blackness slowly and gently blew across a field exposing a community of peasant farmers plowing the land by hand. Time and space had once again morphed. Years, decades, centuries flew as quickly as the miles between there and here. From when she once was to who she was now, still the same person, just older. Zabella did not recognize this place, or the people dressed in their strange garb.

"Stop resisting and just accept what you see. This is what you came to learn." Rehema's voice echoed with anger in the wind. "Now, pay attention, this is an important time in my mother's life. It will be an important time in yours now. This is what your precious Aberash should have shown you. I supposed the shape of the world is as much her fault for releasing the creatures as it is for what she introduced to men."

Rehema's words hurts as they were meant to. Zabella had yet to see what all this had to do with her or how it would serve her. She now knew the dragons could be captured and chained. How they were imprisoned was yet to be shown. Apollonia did not seem to be able to do so. Perhaps it was Aberash who discovered that secret. If she did, why not tell her. Why didn't Rehema tell her?

"Patience! You either know everything or you know nothing. You are facing more than you can image. You must understand your foes and friends."

Her appearance had changed slightly. Her eyes deeper set, more focused and fuller of wisdom. Her face was harder, stern and purposeful. Her features were of a person who spent her life searching for what could not be found. A quest that brought her here, now. Zabella was getting accustomed to the thoughts and feelings of Apollonia, and feeling Rehema's influence less, just a faint distant touch in her mind.

The field stretched for miles from the river's edge to within a few feet of the city's wall. Ditches, a yard deep, ran across the field from the river to a larger, deeper gully that was parallel to the river and ended in a well. Narrow and shallow irrigation ditches extended from the deeper ones and ran through the fields at regular intervals. Men, women, and children worked sharpened iron rods driven through heavy oak arms at the midpoint. Each arm had two wagon wheels, half the height of a man, on either side at the front end. A long pole ran through the wheels and the pivot point of the arm connected four plows two feet apart. The youngest children were strapped into wicker baskets just in front of the iron spikes to add weight. The men, women, and older children lifted a second pole which passed through the other end of the arms and pushed. The families were in the midst of the spring planting season. Hundreds of acres of wheat, oats, barley, potatoes, and carrots had to be planted before the Spring Rains arrived.

The land was hard and dry, not just from the long winter, but from the lack of water flowing down from the mountain. Some of the town's people walked ahead of the plows with buckets of water from the well, wetting the ground. Each bucket was less than half full and the water barely softened the land. Over the last three years the river level had been falling, which in turn meant less water in the irrigation streams that fed Avejion's fields.

Napoli had been keeping a record of the water levels; the previous year had produced the worst harvest in his memory. "If the spring rains does not restore the river to its prior state, we will have to travel up the mountain to find the blockage. Last winter, we came very close to exhausting our winter storage!"

"Do not fear, my husband," Viola shouted back, "God will provide all that is needed. This is His land, and He shall not leave us to perish upon it. We are good people, and He favors us."

Napoli smiled at his wife. Her golden hair wrapped and flowing down her back formed its own river. Her eyes were bright and full of hope and faith. "If only God would take the sweat off our backs and water our fields. Then I would not worry."

Viola regarded the shimmering body of her shirtless husband. He was broad-chested and tall. His arms took most of the weight of the driver pole. His legs rippled as he pushed the plow forward. Every step marked by a droplet of sweat. "If God sent us the Deluge of Noah you would still find cause to worry, my Love."

"Even more a cause for concern," laughed Napoli, "that would be more water than any of us would ever wish for. But, as for God caring for His good people, I have not seen nor heard from Pierre, nor any of his people of the mountain in two years now. And what's more, trapping in the foothills was virtually nonexistence this winter. You know we had to travel for two days to trap even the meager meat we brought back. Ever since the thundering in the mountain three years ago things have been changing, and not to our favor."

"You worry too much about God's business. Just push the driver and do what needs to be done." Viola glanced first at her last-born, Victoria, in her basket, then passed her gaze to the mountains in the distance. She too, worried when the thunder rolled day and night there, but no rain fell. But it had settled down and whatever evil had descended upon the people of the mountain, it concerned Pierre and his people, not them. Viola was a caring and kind-hearted woman, but in harsh times she had to focus her strength on her family, her friends, and her city. Pierre and his people would do the same. If they were in need of their assistance, Pierre would have come to the city to seek it. The mountain people were proud, but they were not foolish.

Napoli could not dismiss the cloudless thunder as easily as his wife. He remembered the tales of his youth. His grandmother instilled in him a Godly amount of fear of the unknown and unexplainable. People who went missing in the night; livestock, the entire herd seemingly plucked from their pastures; cities and towns completely decimated; mindless armies coming out of nowhere to kill without purpose; she had a story for each. She summoned all these things up in one word, Dragons. Spawns of the Devil sent to destroy and cause misery across the world. Although she knew not where they came from, or for that matter, had never seen one in her lifetime, she warned him about the signs of evil among them. An angry mountain, vanishing food supply, nature herself rebelling against mankind, these were signs the Evil One was at work nearby.

His wife simply attributed the lack of water and rumblings to landslides. Not a usual occurrence but one that happened from time to time. Ice and snow upon the mountain, an unfortunate turn of nature, and the river could become dammed. Even something less malevolent, as beavers had blocked the river at narrow turns more than once. A beaver dam could become quite a formidable obstacle over the years, but hardly the work of the Devil. She knew there was always a logical explanation for the things men readily attributed to the supernatural. A handful of men with axes and shovels needed to venture up the mountain to clear the river at its source. So, after the hard work of plowing the fields was done, several of the men would ascent the mountain.

I t was just after supper. The sun had set. The fires had been set in the towers of the city walls. The walls were thick and old, taller than any house, built in the time of the Romans. There were square towers five hundred feet apart on each side of the wall and circular towers at the four corners. The walls surrounded the city, enclosing and protecting its citizens from dangers long forgotten. Each wall had a single arched gateway built into the center towers tall enough for mounted horsemen to pass through at least four abreast.

Avejion had no such garrison these days. The gates were heavy iron bars, thick as a man's leg with space between them only a child's arm could squeeze through which rolled into the wall between the outer and inner stones. Gigantic wooden wheels mounted on either side behind the walls needed to be turned to open and close the gates. The guards could turn either wheel to operate the gate, however they moved easiest when both were turned in unison. The gates were left open most of the time. The walls and gates had protected the city for centuries with little need for upkeep.

The first watchmen took their positions in the watchtowers at the onset of dusk. Practice kept alive from time immemorial, although of little use today in these peaceful times. Avejion held no strategic significance in the French kingdom.

The men gathered in the Common House in the town square. They waited for Napoli to begin. He had become the unofficial leader of Avejion. His knowledge of the planting seasons, his ability to read the signs, and wisdom beyond a man his age should hold, made him trusted even among the elders. If Napoli said they needed to have a meeting, no one questioned his reasons as to why. They all gathered in the Common House around their family tables, the Clevers, the Vesies, the Arrons, the Masse, and a dozen more all drawing brew from the kegs and waiting for Napoli. His twin brothers sat at the Napoli family table, the last of their line.

Napoli was on his way, having tucked his three golden haired daughters into bed with a frightful story of witches. His wife kissed him passionately then scolded him thoroughly, "why do you tell them such stories. They will be awake again within an hour with night terrors. And you, my husband, will be consoling yourself and the other men with mead and ale."

"Drinking a bit is to be sure but consoling each other is hardly the order of this night. We must make provisions to enter the mountains and find the source of the blockage. The spring rain has come and as dark as the skies have been over the mountains, the river is still a little more than a gentle brook. What has fallen on our plains will sprout the crops, but we need a continuous flow to bring it to bear. I told the girls a story so they would not be left to wonder what befell their father as I was left to ask the same questions about my father when he climbed the Eastern Mountains."

"That was nearly a decade ago," Viola stroked his hair back, "surely you don't still believe any more than an unfortunate step took him."

"A dozen men went into the mountains to hunt, all expert bowmen, and none returned. Another two-dozen searched for them along all the hunting trails and no sign of my father, or the others were found. A single death is an accident; an entire party goes missing is a mystery to be solved. The only answers I can perceive that would claim the bodies and souls of a dozen able men is a darkness, not of this world, befell them. Now, I will climb those same mountains to find what claims our water and seeks to destroy us, whole and completely."

"Jacques Napoli, may I have a word?" asked a person in a dark-hooded cloak from the shadows. The voice was of a woman, but he didn't recognize it. She was standing between Masse's house and barn. He felt compelled to stop and answer her.

"Who are you? Show yourself." Napoli commanded.

The woman stepped into the moonlight and dropped her hood. Her eyes sparkled, as did her skin and hair. She moved closer to him, and he felt he should withdraw but was held in place. A strange force made his body go stiff. She spoke softly, "I'm sorry for using my powers on you but I must protect myself. If I have your word that you will not attack me or call out, I will release you."

Napoli just thought his acceptance and his body became his

own once again. "Witch, what do you want from me? I'm a simple farmer. I have nothing of worth to give you."

"I want nothing from you. I am here to help you. You are planning to go into the mountains, and you will need me as a guide."

"How do you know my mind? Where are you from? You are not from the mountains, nor from the nearby towns."

"You are right, I am from far away. But what you will find in the mountains will take what I know for you to survive."

"My Grandmother told me, 'First comes the thunder, then the witches, and finally the black cloud of fire.' And nothing good can be had whence that happens."

"I am Apollonia. I have waited five hundred years for this dragon to show himself. He has begun to build his power once again. From this day forward only misery and death shall befall you and your people."

"Dragon! I am going to find out what is blocking the river. Not going to fight a dragon. I can't tell those men we are going to battle a dragon."

Apollonia knew that Jacques Napoli was vaguely aware of what awaited him in the mountains, even if he didn't want to put a name to it. The dragon had been working his way west and was about to claim everything from the mountains to the sea. She needed his strength to lead a small band of men to defeat it before he came to true power. "Then don't tell them. They think they are going to unblock a river and that is what they are going to do. But know this, what is blocking the river is a castle and its dragon. You have felt his presence for a long time now. If you go up the mountain, and you know you must, you will need my help if you plan to come back down."

"Why should I trust you, witch? You attack me from the shadows with your magic."

"You need not fear me," Apollonia stepped closer and put a

hand on Jacques' chest. "We have a common enemy. All mankind has but one foe to fight, and I have been waiting a long time for someone of your nature to lead the battle. Your heart is true, and you know mine is too." Apollonia stepped back into the shadows and Jacques' eyes betrayed him as she seemed to shrink and fade away.

As Napoli walked into the Common House, he was greeted by shouts and cheers. The men had been drinking and wondering what was on Jacques Napoli's mind this night. He passed through the crowd more somber than any had seen him before. Shaking hands and accepting slaps on the shoulder until he reached the kegs and drew himself a large wooden pint of ale. He drank it down and drew a second immediately. Jacques' plan had changed drastically after talking to Apollonia. He had planned on taking twenty men up the mountains to the source of the river. Now, he knew he would need a lot more if they were to face a dragon. And he had agreed not to tell the others of the true danger.

First, he felt the men would laugh him out of the Common House. He doubted if any, even the elders, had ever seen a dragon. Everyone had heard stories of dragons, but they were just that, stories. Most believed they were folk tales. Something mothers told their children to coerce obedience from them, "bad children are carried off in the night by sharp claws and made a meal for the evil ones, mind your manners and do your chores."

Second, he knew these men and their families. They would not be eager to lay down their lives. And he couldn't blame them, from the stories of his grandma, facing a dragon was certain death. A horrible way to die. Death by fire or eaten alive was the fate he would offer them. So instead, he said, "the blockage is probably bigger than what I thought. I need fifty able-bodied men to come with me."

Peter, the older of the twin brothers by seven minutes, asked, "why do you think it is such a big blockage?"

"It has been building for years now. The winter ice and rocks have locked up the river. We are going to have to move a lot of rocks and the more men the quicker and easier will be the job."

"I can build a lever and pulleys to move the rocks with less effort," Paul the younger twin offered.

"You two are not coming."

The room erupted in protest. The twins and others pointed out that they had reached adulthood a year ago, it was time for them to do the work of men. The twins, the most adamant.

Jacques countered their arguments, "you two are only fourteen and have not taken wives."

"We are moving rocks, not going to war," argued Peter.

"You may have the brawn of our father," added Paul, "but I have the brains of our mother. You need me if you are to move even one stone!"

The Common House erupted in laughter, everyone cheering on the two brothers. Jacques was the head of his family and well within his rights to bar the pair from participating, but reluctantly, he allowed them to join the expedition. Fifty more volunteered and all agreed to leave in a month, as the weather would be warmer and the ice would be less of a problem. Napoli requested the town's forge to turn out six-foot iron spikes and fifty-pound mallets. Also, chains with links as thick as his fist were forged. These items were implanted in his mind by Apollonia.

He felt her influence as he went about town setting up the trip. She had gone from the town that same night but never from his thoughts. He could feel her directing his actions. And her eyes invaded his dreams. As did the visions of flame-like clouds and rivers of fire. Over the next few weeks, Jacques woke in sweats and shaking.

Viola admonished him, "serves you right for frightening the girls like you do. You shall see I am right. There is nothing to fear in the mountains but falling rocks and dead trees."

"And what of Pierre and his people? What has become of them?"

Viola stared out the window at the moon crossing the mountaintops. Deep lines etched her face, but she tried to force a smile for the sake of her husband. "The lack of water drove the game away. He's a good leader; he would have followed the food wherever it may have gone."

T hey left at daybreak with two loaded wagons. One carried a hundred feet of chains, a dozen spikes, and some things Paul said they had to bring. It was also loaded with swords and shields for each member of the team. They thought it was odd to bring weapons but accepted it as precautionary equipment. The second wagon carried food and drink, of course.

A day into the journey Apollonia joined them. Napoli told the men she would guide them through the mountains. The men objected; all agreeing she looked too old to survive the journey. But no one had ever been further into the mountains than a few miles up the foothills. This journey would take them to the snow line or further. Only she had crossed the mountains and was dressed for the cold temperatures. Napoli hunted in the mountains, as had all the men, so they had packed cloaks, but nothing that would protect them from the frigid air for long. They all hoped it would be over quickly.

Apollonia struck the men as odd. Her white hair and frail body did not match her strength and abilities. She was exceptional on horseback, carried her weapons and shield at all times without tiring, and ate less than anyone else. She was awake before the men, and no one ever saw her sleep. A few days into the journey the men confronted Napoli. Not directly, but by asking the twins to speak with him. They had one question on their mind.

"Is she a witch?" Paul asked, as he watched Apollonia walk out of the camp after sunset, as she did many nights. "Why do we need her to clear a blocked river?"

"She is," Jacques answered his brothers bluntly. "Don't tell the others…"

"The others already suspect as much," declared Peter. "We are only trying to find out if you are under her spell."

"No. She has not cast any dark magic on me."

"How would you know?" questioned Paul.

"My mind is clear. My thoughts are my own. Let me continue, but this is what you must keep amongst ourselves."

"I don't like this, Jacques. These are our friends. They trust you with their lives," Peter's concern was written on his face.

"Let him speak," said Paul softly, even as the others kept their distance, "then we will decide if the others need to know what Jacques and the Witch are planning."

"It's true, these men are our friends, and I would trade my life for any one of theirs. But if they knew the true danger we will face in the mountains, they may turn back now. And I wouldn't blame a single man for doing so. But I need their arms to fight…" Jacques grabbed each brother by the shoulder as if to stop them from fleeing.

"Just speak the truth," Paul implored. The look of terror in his oldest brother's eyes unnerved him.

"What is blocking the river is a dragon!" Napoli felt a great weight lift from him. Just speaking the words made the night a little brighter. It was like he awoke from a dream that he had been trapped in ever since meeting Apollonia.

The two brothers laughed.

"Are you trying to make fools of us? Or has this witch really enchanted you and you are now incapable of seeing the truth?" Peter couldn't believe they were having this conversation. But the look on Jacques's face let him know his brother was steadfast in his conviction. "What makes you think there is a dragon in the mountains?"

"I have seen it." Napoli knew his brothers were shocked by the statement. He could see in their eyes they wanted to burn Apollonia at the stake and drag him back to town tied to a log. No matter what he told them now, however unbelievable, it would decide the outcome of this journey. "Apollonia has shown me the beast. She has a way of reaching into my thoughts and sharing what she has been through. She has tried to kill the creature before, but without the aid of men, such as ourselves, she cannot do it. And we must do it now, as his power is growing. By this time next year, he will be upon us."

"And you still believe you are not under some dark spell. I think we should put him to the test," Paul smirked. "We hold him over the flames and see if his words catch fire. Then we will know if he is truly bewitched or speaking the truth."

"Be serious! If this all be truth," Peter said earnestly, "fifty-two men will be no match for a dragon. You should have raised an army."

"She had an army," Napoli told them, "She had many armies. They fought and died. Therefore, we cannot tell the others. Apollonia believes a small group; a few men can challenge and defeat the dragon with spikes and chains."

"I still think you may be bewitched, but we will keep this a secret for now," Paul spoke for his twin as well, "although, it will be wise to inform the others before they come face to face with your dragon. If you think they may flee now, imagine the reaction of facing something like that without warning."

"When the time is right, I will tell all what is needed to be known."

The three were about to join the camp when a black horse whinnied and appeared. It was pulling a wagon driven by two women. Something strange followed the wagon and as it was almost upon them it took the form of Apollonia. The wagon rolled past them barely making a sound. The two women were young, slightly older than the twins. They appeared to be twins also, with long black hair and dark narrow colorless eyes that slanted upward in a peculiar fashion. Their skin was white as moonlight.

Apollonia broke the men's trance, "they will aid us in fighting the dragon and his ogres. They bring something that is very useful in confronting dragon's fire."

"Ogres?" Peter questioned. "We have heard of dragons. I

don't believe in them. Just old tales my grandmother used to tell us. But what on earth is an ogre?"

"They are foul beasts. Not yet a dragon, but more than a man. Very powerful, very dangerous. The good news is we can kill them. It won't be easy, but it can be done."

Peter and Paul looked at Jacques stunned.

He returned their stare then said, "not a word of this to the others."

The men accepted the two strange women as they had accepted Apollonia. One witch or three it made no difference anymore. They reached the foothills and were greeted by a wind which carried the stench of death on it. Looking up towards its jagged peaks, the mountains showed no signs of life. The green trees had withered. The forest had become a land of spikes, forbidding anyone to enter. The land was chalky and brown. All the grass had died and long blown away; dirt and rock were left behind. The sky above was a mosaic of gray and black clouds. Everyone knew there was something evil in the mountains.

They spent another day travelling over the barren lands of the foothills. There were no sounds, no birds, nor insect chatter. The sounds of wagon wheels crushing dirt and stones beneath their heavy load filled the men's ears. Their horses breathed softly as if they were trying not to stir the air. Fear gripped man and beast alike. It had a strangle hold upon their throat and was slowly tightening its fingers. They marched on in silence, no one dared to voice what was on his mind. Mostly out of dread their witchy companions would invade their souls. At the wide passage leading into the mountain, they heard a long, tortured cry which sent shivers down every spine. It didn't emanate from any bird or animal the men knew. "What in God's Holy Name was that?" Jacques asked.

"That was an ogre," answered Aberash, one of the twin witches, in a hushed tone. "They know we are here and what we have come for."

"I liked it better when I thought we were going to clear rocks," Paul whispered to Peter.

CHAPTER 5

INTO THE HIGHLANDS

N ightfall at the foot of the mountains, Napoli and Apollonia began to make their plans. The rest of the men were in a deep sleep in their tents. A sleep he was sure was induced by the women.

"We need to get the wagons to the upper mountain pass," Appolonia said.

"The paths are solid, but they narrow pass the high pines," Jacques informed her. "But the forest is less dense, or so it seems. We may be able to drive the horses a good distance before having to carry the equipment ourselves."

"It is imperative we get the barrels my daughters brought to the top," Appolonia told him without elaborating further, although the inquisitive look from Jacques begged for more. "I will find the best and quickest way tonight. There is much danger ahead, many eyes upon us, if they know what we are bringing, they will descend upon us in force."

She turned to Aberash. *If I fail to return…*

You will not fail, Mother. Your powers are strong, and we will aid you.

We do not know what the dragon has laid before us. Warned

Appolonia. *You must be ready to take charge. You are strong enough to lead, and these men will follow you. The dragon must not leave this mountain. Trust Napoli, he has strength of heart. Use his power to supplement yours.*

Avia and I will not fail you, Mother.

J acques Napoli watched a bizarre ritual between the three women. They chanted and swayed in the moonlight. The two younger witches stroked Apollonia with stones and jewels they carried in pouches.

Apollonia began to shrink and twist. Her white hair grew and covered her body, And her clothes fell from her sliming form. She dropped to the ground as her arms and legs deformed. They thinned and lengthened, hands and feet, fingers and toes receded. She howled and took on the shape of a timber wolf. The transformation came effortlessly to Apollonia thanks to her daughters.

Larger than any wolf Jacques had seen, he knew she wanted him to witness the transformation, but he wasn't sure why. *Can she be trying to gain my confidence or is she drawing me deeper into her spell?*

Apollonia gave another howl and dashed off through the dead forest.

The quickest way to the top was on all fours, but she must be careful to avoid the ogres. There was thunder above her, ogres reacting to her presence. The mountains were wrapped in a milky fog. The maidens' powers had taken control of the weather to give her an edge over the physical prowess of the ogres. They sat with Jacques; arms locked in a circle around a glowing pile of gemstones. The two's eyes were bright as if a fire had burned behind them. Jacques felt queer ruminations/rumblings? from the ground beneath him coursing through his body and into the other two. He heard strange voices singing in his head, and the wind howled although there was no breeze upon his skin. The witches needed his presence to complete their triad, even if he had no idea what he was doing. They used his physical prowess to sustain and project their powers into the night.

In the five hundred years she had been searching, she had learned many things. Ogres had the night vision of a hawk and the sense of smell of a hog. Wolf form was best for what she needed to do. She was quick and sure-footed, able to slip past them with ease. Running close to the ground, under brushes, her black and white fur a coat of camouflage. Creatures turned quickly at the sound of a pebble rolling down the mountain's path. Their heads jerking upward as they caught a faint whiff of hair. Apollonia moved as a shadow and spirit through the darkness and dense fog.

And when the mountain opened to the full brightness of the moonlit night, she pushed the thought of her presence from the ogres' mind. Usually, single-minded in their focus of guarding their master throughout the night, she easily turned their attention to their stomach. Hunger was their weakness. They needed enormous amounts of food for their massive bodies.

She made it up and down before sunrise. Napoli was waiting for her. He hadn't slept all night but was fully alert. He felt even more vibrant having spent the night in a trance with the two sisters. He now knew these women as mermaids who had travel from the Mediterranean Sea and beyond. Those who men called witches were not women possessed by evil spirits, but beings like men and dragons. Ancient and exotic, but not evil, they helped mankind and protected the world from the true evil. Aberash and Avia were twins like his brothers but born ten years apart to Apollonia. The mermaids were also known as maidens by those who travelled the seas because they were born without sexual encounters. They were pure of spirit and body.

Each had her own unique powers that flooded into Jacques through the night. Aberash's mind was more powerful than her mother's. She could control a man in an instant. Make him do things without his knowledge. Avia was a benevolent soul. She took away pain and healed broken bodies and spirits. Apollonia had chosen him for this task because he was strong-willed and had a firm mind. Many men would not be able to withstand a mental bonding with a mermaid. They would become so enthralled with the woman they could not function. They needed him to be able to bond with the two of them, and maybe all three before this was over. He was determined. His will was like iron. He proved to be up to the task.

Jacques learned they were in what was known to the maidens as the Second Split. A great war being fought by dragons, maidens, and men. It had started millennia ago when the first dragon, Ehecatl, decided to create more dragons and divided the world between the four of them. Deyhezas and Vargrerot were part of the four, and for a time, each was content in his own part of the world. But their greed and hunger for flesh and power could not be satisfied. They turned men against each other for sport and pleasure. Then they turned on each other. Each dragon determined to kill his brothers, claim his power, and become the sole ruler of the world. To win, they created less powerful dragons, who in turn were determined to take over from their creators. This was the world they were in now. "Did you find your dragon?"

"I wasn't looking for the dragon," Apollonia said, transforming out of her animal form. "I know where he is. He lives in an aerie atop the mountain. I was looking for his protection. And a way to get to him without detection."

"Well, what did you find?"

"As I expected, there are three ogres on the high ridge."

"I thought mermaids only changed into fish," Jacques said once Apollonia was fully human and dressed.

"Not a fish, but in our natural form we belong to the sea. But that would not suit us here, would it? We can bond with the spirit of many creatures and thus take on its shape," Apollonia explained, "including humans as you see me now. But there are limits, nothing too small, as say a mouse, after all I would be a rather large mouse."

"Then why not take the shape of the eagle and fly over the mountain terrain? You would have gained a much better vantage point in less time."

"We never take the form of any winged creature, that would

bring us too close in nature to the dragons. It would expose us in mind and body to an attack. You just experienced fully bonding with us. Can you imagine how devastating it would be for me to be joined to a dragon? The evil that flows through them would be overwhelming. I saw all I needed to see from the ground. The dragon commands a small army of men from both sides of the mountain. You know some of them, the man in charge is called Pierre."

Napoli had known his childhood friend was still alive, he had felt it in his heart. They had developed a bond over the years that transcended mere friendship. They had become like brothers even before Peter and Paul were born. Their fathers had taken them hunting and trapping. The mountain people and the plainsmen enjoyed a good and symbiotic relationship. Jacques' father, Vincent, believed in fair and honest dealings with all his neighbors. Constantine, Pierre's father, believed the same. They quickly came to an understanding, Vincent and his men would be allowed to hunt deer and bear every full moon, and smaller animals whenever they wanted. Constantine received three wagon loads at harvest time. As a symbol of their agreement, Constantine delivered twenty heads of goats to the city and Vincent gave two male calves and a heifer.

When Jacques turned eight years of age, he accompanied his father and the other men on his first hunting party. Constantine and Pierre joined them on that special occasion. Constantine was very tall, and carried a bow as tall as Jacques, and a quill of black-tipped arrows half his size. Pierre had his own bow and arrow set, having been hunting for two years. His bow was also taller than he was, but he bragged, "I can draw an arrow more than half length and take down a full-grown buck."

On the first night the party of twelve crept up to the clearing alongside a tidal pool where the main river took a bend around some boulders and across the flat rocky terrain. They were perched between the trees above and downwind where deer came to drink. They didn't wait long before a buck led a trio of does and five fawns out. Constantine rose slowly to his feet drawing the bow to full arrow length in one fluid silent motion. A muted zip sliced through the air as the obsidian arrowhead flew toward the buck. A dull thump proceeded the buck's cry and it kicked up and ran into the forest. "Go after him, boys! He should leave a blood trail easy to follow."

Jacques and Pierre jumped to their feet and sprang down the narrow path.

Constantine yelled after Jacques, "And when you return, this bow and quill will be waiting for you."

"That is a large stag you hit," Vincent said, "those two boys will never be able to drag it back here."

"I know. We give them a few minutes and then we go after them." Constantine then pulled the cork from his goatskin and offered him a drink of wine. "You allowed me the first kill, you, my friend, can have the first drink."

"Thanks, but you are our host, the first arrow is always yours. And I think this may not be your first drink either. I remember you bringing down a stag twice as large where it stood," joked Vincent then swallowed a large amount of wine.

"Ah, but where is the thrill in that," he replied taking his turn on the flask. "This is your boy's first hunt; he should feel the excitement of the kill. And learn when it is right to do so, and when it is not. Do not worry, that stag will not go far. I just hope the life does not run out of it before the boys can catch up to it."

"Did you see the way they took off after it," Vincent laughed, "talk about excited. I'm sure they will catch it in full gallop."

The boys were fast, but the buck was quicker. Crashing through the forest, it was easier to follow the sound than the trail of blood in the dark. The chase lasted ten minutes before the animal fell silent ahead of them. It lay on its side in a thicket breathing heavily and bellowing a low mournful sound. Pierre whispered, "why do they always pick the thorniest place to die?"

"Probably hoping we would be discouraged and leave it in peace."

"It is facing the wind. Get your knife ready," commanded Pierre, "my father said the kill is to be yours. I will circle around in front of him, keep his attention while you come from behind and put your blade to his throat. You have slit an animal's throat before?"

"Of course, I have," Jacques said with confidence. "I am the oldest son. I have butchered the goats."

"Well, this is a lot bigger than your goats. And bigger horns as well."

Jacques lifted his shirts exposing a long and jagged scar on his right side. "Goats don't like the knife at their throat either."

The boys took their places. The stag snorted loudly as the thickets crackled behind its head. Pierre stomped on a bush making his own snapping sounds as Jacques advanced slowly. Finally, Jacques reached his hand out and stroked the neck down to the beast's shoulder. It shook its head and Jacques ducked a pointy antler. He reached out again, and this time laid his body across the buck, careful to avoid the wound in its side below the shoulder.

"What are you doing?" Pierre shrieked.

"I learned from the goats; it is easier to draw a blade across the throat if the animal is calm and at peace."

"Oh, that's interesting," Pierre said trying to keep his tone low and even. "I should warn you; it may only be catching its wind and could charge me at any moment now. So, please get on with it."

Jacques obliged and stuck the eight-inch knife blade into the middle of the buck's neck halfway between the head and chest and quickly ripped backwards, falling off the animal. Blood flowed into the thicket. "Done."

Jacques saw his father, Constantine, and the other men standing a few yards off. They began laughing as he moved slowly and carefully from the thorns. They came forward with swords and axes to cut through the thicket and pull the buck out. Vincent turned his son's face from side to side inspecting the scratches and cuts inflicted by the thorns, "Next time, you can wait for it to die."

"Maybe, next time your strike will be better than mine," Constantine said and handed the boy his bow.

"I do not think so," Jacques said wide-eyed. He ran his hands up the side of the bow, amazed at the soft smoothness of it. The bow's grip was small and curved, just right to fit his hand. The arrow rest had a slight bend towards the riser to keep the arrow steady. It rose flattish before a half twist of the belly and flat back. The recurve of the upper and lower limb was pure white in contrast to the darker tan of the rest of the bow. "What kind of wood is this?"

"Not wood. Deer antler," informed Constantine, "I carved it from the first buck Pierre killed, he wanted you to have it. Took me two years, but you will still have to give it a name and its first kill."

"Thank you. Thank you, both," Jacques said to Pierre and his father. "My father gave me a crossbow to use on this hunt."

"A crossbow is for war. I saw how you calmed the buck before finishing him, a bow is a weapon of mercy. You practice with it, and you will be able to bring down your prey with one strike where it stands, and you can stay out of the thickets." They all laughed.

It had been years since he had seen Pierre or anyone from his tribe. They started disappearing just as the water did. Pierre told him the animals were becoming scarce and his people had to hunt at higher altitudes to find game. His hunters would go out and never return.

Apollonia told him most of the men were put to work cutting the dragon's castle into the face of the mountain. But the ogres had undoubtedly eaten some of the women and children as sustenance. They blocked the river purposely to bring his men into the mountain. She told Napoli that the dragon now needed his people for his army. "He will use his mental powers to frighten and coerce your people into his service. Those who do not bend to his will are going to forfeit their lives."

"What can we do against a dragon? I was told a dragon cannot be killed."

"Not necessarily true, Jacques. Another dragon can kill one, and I know a man trapped one, I believe a man may be able to kill one with the proper weapons. However, we need to reach its lair first, which means you must fight your friend. And kill him."

These words weighted heavy on his heart. If his friend was under the power of a dragon, he wanted to free him, not kill him. But he still had to get past his friend.

Jacques pulled Merci, the bow he was given as a boy, from the wagon and unwrapped the buckskin covering. He took the quiver which was also made from buckskin and pulled all the obsidian arrows out. He laid them in the buckskin wrap in the wagon and left the sharpened wood tipped arrows in the holder. "If we are to face them in battle, we will not take their lives. We will free them from the grip of the beast. The men need to know that we may have to fight these people," Jacques said, dismayed. "They are friends and share kinship with them. Some of our people have married and moved to the mountain, and some of theirs have joined us. I am not the only one who will find it difficult to raise arms against our brothers."

"As you wish," agreed Apollonia, "we may be able to aid you in this noble endeavor. But mind you, we must not fail to reach the dragon's lair. And we will need all that we have brought to defeat him." And she opened his eyes to what she had witnessed.

The mountain people patrolled the trees just below the falls. They walked in pairs, without words or expressions. One carried a sword in hand, the other a crossbow locked and loaded. They marched along the trails in an endless nonstop parade. Every few minutes another pair would go by, seemingly blind to their surroundings.

"The dragon sees through their eyes and relays their visions to the ogres. Pierre's people are his sentinels as well as his army.

He commands a larger force that he will bring to bear if we are detected," warned Apollonia.

The way up the mountain was by crossing the waterfalls, but it was not the only way. As kids, Jacques and Pierre found caves behind the falls which led into the mountain and came out above the ridgeline. The caves were huge, wide, and high enough to bring the wagons through. This would be the path they would take, once they got past Pierre's men.

CHAPTER 6

FRIENDLY FOES

The men came upon a rock dam in the river. It was five feet high and a couple of feet thick. It stretched from one side of the riverbank to the other.

This was not the work of beavers, Jacques surmised.

Some of the men began unloading the spikes and ropes from the wagon.

"What are you doing?" questioned Apollonia.

"What we came here to do," replied one of the men indignantly. "We are going to clear this blockage."

"Why? The water behind these rocks is only ankle deep. Surely you don't think this is what's keeping your fields dry."

"We should clear every blockage we come to until the water flows freely," the burly bearded man replied and then turned to Jacques, "am I right?"

We must keep moving. There is great danger ahead. This is a trap to slow us down and possibly ambush us. We must reach the mountain peaks before nightfall.

"Jerasso, it would make more sense to find and destroy the major dam first, then with the power of the river behind us, we can clear these little ones on our way back," Jacques told his friend.

Jerasso, the blacksmith, didn't agree but felt the need to move on. Since entering the mountains, a dark presence surrounded them. The purpose of their mission may not be to move rocks from the river, after all, as Jacques had told them. The three witches and their barrels of wine they said were to trade for water rights if the mountain people refused to let them remove the dams were surely a farce. Hearing the strange sounds in the mountains and witnessing the lack of life around them, this mission was becoming less about water and more about an impending battle. The weapons they had brought, he refashioned in a way he did not know. How did Jacques, a farmer, know about cooking and adding coal to the iron ore? Or that using a small enclave to preheat air and forcing it into the kiln would produce weapons that were stronger and sharper. The gleaming forged iron was lighter and better to use, and for chains and spikes too, but for what purpose? Jacques never answered that question.

Perchance, Jacques didn't know the answers to the questions no one dared give voice to. But Jerasso could see it in his eyes and those of his three witchy women that there were more than rocks to attend to in the mountain. There was a possibility that Jacques only truly knew that whatever was blocking the river's flow would not give way without a fight. Exactly what they would be fighting had yet to be determined or revealed. Jacques had made clear the uncertainty of the venture back in the Common House. Maybe, if Jacques had confided the facts he did know in the beginning, none of them would have come this far. But he, as did the others, gave their word to follow this mission to its end. If water flow was only the final outcome, with other ominous motives and conclusions to be achieved, Jerasso knew they could not turn back without seeing it done.

The thunder that rolled day and night, with or without clouds, were war drums driving them onward. Only by not knowing with certainty what awaited them ahead could Jerasso convince himself to climb higher. Here in the mountains, he thought the answers were near. He felt eyes upon him. And sensed the dread that waited for them.

"We may not have to kill these people," Napoli told Apollonia. "You have the power to cloud their minds, I know this is true. I can feel your thoughts in my head."

"I may be able to block their knowledge of your men's advance," confirmed Apollonia. "I had planned to do that; it is the only way you will be able to defeat them. There are three hundred men, without blinding them to your presence they would slaughter you easily. I sense no compassion, no moral restraint, nothing that will stop your old friend from ending your life. He hears only his master's voice, and he must obey."

"If we must fight, we will," Jacques relented, "but give me another way to get by them without drawing blood."

The maidens formed the Triad, each sitting cross-legged in a circle of sacred stones. They placed two fingers on each other's temples and began chanting and swaying. Their voices carried on the wind. It became the wind; the trees swayed in harmony. Jacques and his men felt an eerie peacefulness and they moved quietly along the road to the waterfalls. The wagons carrying the witches, irons, and supplies rolled silently on the dirt path. Time slowed; seconds turned to minutes in the minds of the men. Their comprehension of the world seemed to twist and shift. Reality bent around them. Their sight stretched far became near, small turned to large. They passed groups of gaunt soulless men. Their eyes black and their heads without thought. They stood like statues in a macabre display of the dead. The men kept a tight grip on their swords, even in this trance the others appeared savage.

Apollonia had warned them not to drop their guard. Pierre's men could break free of the hypnotic effect of the siren song at any time. She pitted her powers against their master's hold on them. The caves were easy to find. The water's flow slowed to the extent that it was a thin silver ribbon pouring down in front of the black hole in the mountain's face. The river was no longer able to hide the entrance to the cave.

There were dozens of men at the opening. The dragon had positioned them there to stop Jacques' men. As they passed the men frozen in a dream, Jacques recognized his friend. He reached out for him. Charles Masse, one of Jacques' best friends, and the man who called all the others together, grabbed Jacques' arm. Great sadness swelled his eyes as he said, "he is beyond your reach now. Best leave him to his Hell, then drag us all in as well."

Jacques knew Charles was right. He too had grown up hunting with them, and also knew Pierre in a better life. What could he do now for his old friend? Break the trance and be forced to run him through with his sword? Perhaps, that was the humane thing to do. But he would jeopardize all their lives by doing so. He hoped once the dragon had fallen, his friend would return to his former life. They entered the cave and exited the daylight.

The cave was voluminous. The ground crackled and shifted beneath their boots. They struck torches and found themselves standing in a bone field. Human and animal bones carpeted the cave's floor. Brittle, they turned to dust with each footstep. Each man sank several inches into the thick flooring. There were too many to be just from the mountain people, Napoli knew the dragon had been feeding here for decades, maybe centuries. He began softly kicking and nudging the bones around his feet.

Careful, Jacques, are you sure you want to find what you are looking for here? Besides, the dragon still listens to the bones. He feels their movement and knows whose feet tread upon them. The dragon prides himself on being aware of all who enter his domain. It's best we keep moving.

"I will lead the way," he said. They marched on; the others greatly disturbed by the bone yard, pushed forward. If his father's bones were among them, best he leaves him to rest in peace. Only the Napoli brothers knew what had such an appetite for so much misery. The deeper they moved into the cave, the more bones they found. Then he noticed the walls had deep gouges running a great distance. At other places the walls were smooth like glass. The light of the flames danced wildly around them. He did not want to spend any more time in the caves than necessary. "Let's hurry. I do not wish to be added to this collection."

All agreed and hastened along. They felt grateful to stand in the daylight once again. A narrow path rose before them. It was steep and the horses would have to go up in a single file. Sunlight bathed the face of the mountain and blinded the men as they pulled the horses and pushed the wagons. The witches walked ahead of the troop. Their powers were less effective on the ogres, but they could be an early warning for the men.

"We must cross the stone bridge up ahead before dark," Apollonia told Jacques. "We do not want to face the ogres at night. They are the most powerful in the dark."

The final climb to the stone bridge was too narrow for the horses and the men almost lost their supply wagon as part of the path crumbled beneath its weight. They took no chances with the irons and the barrels the witches had brought. They unloaded them and passed the wooden kegs hand to hand up the hundred feet of the sheer cliff wall. Then they dragged the heavy chains as close to the walls as physically possible. One slip and the weight of the chains would have yanked them to their death. Finally, they pulled the empty wagons up and reloaded them on the plateau before the bridge. It took most of the day to reach this point. They had at best, an hour of daylight remaining.

Apollonia hurried the men out onto the stone bridge which connected the top of one mountain peak to another. Carved long ago by the wind that still howled around the peaks, the bridge had been created hundreds of years before when the face of the mountain collapsed into a mile deep gorge. It formed the two peaks, and the thick granite spanned between them. The bridge became the natural creation of ice, rain, wind, and the heat of the sun. But more recently, rock walls have been built along each side of the expanse. Probably to keep the less sure-footed users from being blown off and down into the abyss.

They could see huge openings cut into the rockface above them. There was one opening that a man on horseback stacked four high could easily pass through. They had reached the castle.

It looked like a face cut into the gray granite mountain, daring them to come forward. It was not a human face. The stone bridge formed part of a tongue extruding from a long snout with rows of teeth. The red glow from within was foreboding and ominous. Atop the face, the peaks and spires formed a crown that forced the eyes down. Legions of soldiers would be hard-pressed against this castle, yet here he was with a few dozen farmers, merchants, tradesmen, and three maidens prepared to do the impossible.

They heard the rush of water somewhere on the other side of the cliffs. Napoli knew the water was being diverted down another face of the mountain, away from its natural course. Away from the people who desperately needed it. Somewhere beyond the face, cut into the rock, was a dam he had to destroy. *I hear the object of our quest in the distance, I know it is not what you have brought us here for. It is not why you are here. How difficult would it be to reach our goal?*

Keep your mind to the task at hand. It will not be easy to achieve, nor will be that of my sisters and I. It is your job to destroy that dam, but first you must reach it, and you are not even close. You are looking at the face of Shabodun. He will not release what he has taken without a fight. It is his pride and ego that has caused him to deform the mountain thus, it will be his downfall, if you can hold onto your courage. He carved this castle to break your will and test your strength.

Apollonia stopped the men when they had ferried the irons, supplies, and half the wooden kegs onto the bridge. "Arm yourselves. Prepare for battle!"

Aberash lit an arrow and let it fly at the dozen kegs left behind at the other end of the bridge. It struck one, and all erupted with a deafening roar. Flames and a shower of rocks rained down on the bridge a few feet away from the men. The cloud of black smoke twisted and rose on the angry wind. Half the stone bridge was gone. Rocks were still tumbling down the mountainside, shaking the troop.

Aberash said as the cacophony died down, "now, there will be no escape."

"Perhaps you forgot," yelled Jacques, "dragons can fly."

"Dragons!" cried the men in a single voice. In that instant, all their fears materialized.

"It is not the dragon whose escape I am preventing," said

Apollonia as thunder echoed from the darkness of the castle. The mountain came to life.

Jerasso stepped forward. The anger in his eyes made his massive arms ripple. He stood face to face with Jacques, ready to crush his skull with a single blow from his fist. "This is the secret you could not share with us?"

"Had I done so, would any of you have journeyed this far?" Jacques defiantly questioned his friend. "Would any of you even venture into the mountains knowing the certainty of death that awaited you? I deceived you because I had to, not because I wanted to. And the deed still needs to be done."

Dragons would not be the first horror the men faced from the mountain castle. A moan loud and painful that the men wished was the wind ripping through the castle, but feared was not, shook them to their core. It left them no time to debate the wisdom of their expedition, or chance to question its outcome. They formed rows, ten across and five deep. What little military training they had sprang forth from forgotten recesses of their youth. As the sounds got louder, Jacques realized that they were coming from more than one source. He suddenly wished he had forced his brothers to stay home. "Any plans for what we will face?"

"Iron spikes to the front," ordered Apollonia. "The ogres do not see well in the bright sunlight. Charge as soon as they emerge."

"So, you have defeated ogres before?" Peter said in a hopeful voice.

"None have ever seen an ogre before and lived" admitted Avia. "But they are slow and ponderous, with a thick hide, but not impenetrable. Strike hard and deep."

As the sounds grew nearer, the men stiffened and prepared to face the unknown. What they faced was totally unexpected to all. The first ogre appeared in the doorway, four times the height of any man there. His eyes burned red and squinted in the sunlight, making them appear like streaks of blood on his hairy face. His burnished skin was thick and hairy too, but he was also covered in armor.

Napoli thought he might be vulnerable to swords and spear in the gaps between its chest and waist. And at the joints of its legs and armpits.

There was intelligence to the thing; he was waiting and sizing them up, formulating a plan of attack. His black, jagged teeth that looked like three rows of saw blades, dripped with saliva. He swung a huge hammer and smashed it down on the ground. The bridge trembled and a chunk from where the end had been blown away crumbled some more. The men froze with fear.

Apollonia knew they would not engage in this battle willingly. And if they waited any longer the ogre would finish them with no trouble. She would have to be the first into battle. She jumped over their heads and landed several feet in front of the terrified men.

Her sisters began chanting and humming loudly.

Apollonia twisted out of her dressings and cried out in pain. Her body stretched and grew. She took on a thick layer of fur, her hands and feet becoming massive paws with three-inch claws. She looked like a bear, but larger than any they had seen. Still, she was less than half the size of the ogre, but it did not deter her. She charged forward on all fours with a mighty roar.

The ogre smashed his hammer once more then ran out onto the bridge to meet Apollonia. A moment before the ogre could swing his hammer, she leaped onto his chest, driving the beast back. Her claws ripped down his chest producing eight rivers of blood. She hung from the armor plates as the ogre shook from side to side trying to cast her off. Finally, she let go and rolled around behind him, then she leaped onto the monster's back, her massive claws gripping him by the neck and shoulders. *What are you waiting for? Attack!*

Napoli's men heeded the command, and all charged forward with spears raised shoulder high. To them, it felt like they were in a nightmare. The giant beast that barred the castle entrance, the white-haired old woman who was now a great bear and spoke to them without words, the howling wind and sounds of anguished souls echoing from deep inside the mountain, all these things were unbelievable, yet true.

The other two women remained behind, casting their spell to empower Apollonia in her battle. She was draining them quickly in this form, but they held onto each other's temple. Blood trickled down the side of their faces as they pressed ever harder. Apollonia grew in size and tore at the back of the ogre. The armor fell from its body and rang out like bells from a cathedral calling to the congregation. The first three men drove their spears into the ogre's stomach but were stopped by the shear bulk of its body. Others slammed into the men to push the spears deeper into the giant. He let out a roar and knocked them away with his hammer.

Lucky for Napoli, Apollonia pulled the beast backward and his swing was weaker than it could have been. The head of the double-sided weapon was half the size of a single man and would have easily crushed their bones on contact. Napoli and his men were piled up along the stone wall of the bridge. The next wave of men charged, running at full speed with spears angled high. The sunlight reflected from the silvery steel spearheads, blinding the ogre, rendering him unable to defend himself from the wave of attackers. Each spearhead was an arm's length, and its wavy design meant to slice through the toughest of flesh. They struck in the same area as their comrades, making use of the wounds in the ogre. They cut deep into their opponent.

Blood gushed forth and drenched the men in green, foul-smelling slime. The ogre bellowed and spat his anger on them. The men stood fast, and more hands grabbed the shafts of the spears. They pushed forward as Apollonia drove the ogre onto their weapons with her massive body. The ogre gave a low growl, more like a moan than a battle cry, and stumbled to the side of the bridge. They mortally wounded the monster, its size less of a weapon than they feared. Ten of the men using the spears and with Apollonia's help shoved the giant beast over the edge of the bridge and down the gorge. Its body slammed on the rocks and bounded down the side of the mountain in an avalanche of stones until it disappeared.

The men cheered their triumph and started towards the door. But their victory was short-lived, a hoard of men armed with lances and swords came charging out of the darkness. A mighty roar and the smell of rotten flesh drove them towards the small band of fighters. Apollonia had already transformed back to a woman. She was too weak to fight and shrank back to her maiden companions in the wagons for safety.

The men quickly formed a wedge of shields and swords, thrusting into the blindly charging hoard. These men were tall, blond, and broad-shouldered. Napoli didn't recognize a single face in the crowd. They were not from this side of the mountain. They wore war paint of strange symbols, slashed at his men wildly and inflicted more injuries to themselves than did his men. They had no battle plan. They swarmed and tried to force their way through and over the shields, impaling themselves on the points of Jacques' men's swords, giving some advantage to the ones who followed. But as Jacques and his band withdrew their blades the wall of men collapsed down, and another thrust would begin the wave buildup again. Jacques and his men gave ground but did not break formation.

As the hordes drove along their flanks, his men forced them, bloody and feeble, over the edge of the stone walls to follow their master, the ogre, into the abyss. Their numbers dwindled swiftly. The few remaining fighters fell to swords and spears before the castle entrance. "What madness drives these people to their death?"

They are all but dead inside their heads, Napoli. Enter carefully, I sense more inside. And there are two more ogres to defeat.

"We will need your magic to kill the ogres," he pleaded with her.

I need time to regain my strength. Aberash and Avia can

guide you, but they will not be able to fight. Open your minds to them and fear not. I did not bring you here to perish.

The inside of the castle opened wide and tall. Columns reached high to the ceilings. Stairs rose and twisted out of sight. Huge arched doorways encircled them and led off in every direction. Torches illuminated the cavernous main hall in a warm and inviting hue. It was quiet. Even the wind had gone silent once they stepped inside the mountain. Peter felt Aberash's thoughts directing him to the left. He tapped his brother's shoulder and a few of the men also turned to follow him. They disappeared down a narrow stairway.

Napoli pointed with his sword across the main hall to a brightly lit hallway. It curved out of sight, but he knew another ogre awaited them at the other end. He took half of the remaining force with him and instructed the others to take positions around the doorway. They armed themselves with spears and waited.

There was a much smaller force of men in the lesser hall. They were more controlled and better fighters. Their eyes were more fluid, as were their movements. They handled their weapons like soldiers and matched Jacques' blow for blow. His advantage was the steel shield that withstood his attacker. And the steel of his sword that shattered the enemy's wooden defenses. One blow split a shield in half and drove its owner backwards. Napoli's men used their shields to corral them. They pushed the group down on the ground and shoved them against the wall. The enemy was covered in oils, so they could squeeze into the rock and chisel the passageways through the mountain. But the oil also made it impossible for them to keep their footing and fight. His men hacked the torches from the walls and their foes writhed and twisted in silent agony as the flames danced on them. A sickness rose inside Jacques' troop as the men were reduced to a mass of groping, burning arms and legs.

Napoli saw a black shadow crawl across the wall and inch its way towards them. It was the second ogre. His shape was indiscernible from his shadow. They braced themselves for whatever was coming their way. Its huge, round face poked through the flames. It had a friendly, almost kind countenance, the bright golden eyes belied the evil in its heart.

Hammolt stood and stamped out the fire with one large thud. The men got splattered with burnt flesh. He smiled as he enjoyed the look of fear in the men. The ogre was twelve feet tall and rotund. He scrapped his one horn that protruded from his forehead along the ceiling, carving a deep rut and dropping boulders to the floor. He smashed them into dust under his eight-hundred-pound hooves. Hammolt was terrorizing the men. His bulky body made it impossible to get behind him. His skin was deep gray leather stretching tight over bulbous masses of muscle and he showed no sign of weakness.

The horn was large, curved upward to a point, and with his head lowered served as a lance. The drawback was that he couldn't track his prey like that. He charged forward, head down, swishing the horn side to side.

The men tumbled over each other in retreat. Hammolt

grabbed one of them in his huge three-fingered hand. Thick boney nails dug into the man's back, and the sound of bone snapping rang out. Hammolt flexed his fingers slightly and the man turned to goo. He licked the man from his hand and smiled again. Then he charged in earnest.

Why did you lead us into this place to die? We should have faced these monsters out in the open. We would have stood a better chance against a demon as huge as this.

Courage men. His great bulk and power would be harder to overcome had he room to put it to better use. Here in this tight confined space his size will be his downfall. Your numbers will overpower him.

The men made an orderly retreat through the passage; they figured the ogre was too big to get to them easily. His horn and claws flung rocks at them as he went. It felled two more men, and he stopped briefly to gobble them up. The men scattered in all directions once out of the confines of the hallway. It confused the ogre, and he did not see the others.

Six men from either side of the doorway charged and drove spears deep into Hammolt's ankles and legs. The joints at the hoof of all animals are mostly bones and tendons, the hide thin and flexible, Hammolt's was no different. He stumbled forward and crashed to the ground. Two more men swung down from lines they had strung between the columns. Their speed gave them the force necessary to pierce the thick hide of the ogre's neck. The six-foot spikes went in one side and out the other.

Hammolt rose slowly to his feet and shook his head, spraying the main hall with blood and green bile. He reached out for Napoli. But his perception was distorted from the blood quickly draining from his brain and Napoli was nowhere near the giant. His blood and slime betrayed him further, sending his massive body smashing back to the floor. As he struggled to regain his footing men rushed in with swords, thrusting at the soft tissues of the golden eyes and fleshy throat. They showed no mercy as they were given none to show.

Hammolt hammered at the men wildly. Blinded by their attack, they easily evaded his massive fists which responded slower and less frequently with each wound inflicted. The men slipped and slid on the slick stone floor but never let up on their assault, determined to make Hammolt pay for the lives he had taken. They stabbed and impaled until Hammolt lay dead still.

Even with two of the dragon's guardians dispatched Jacques still doubted the wisdom of the women and this battleplan. *Apollonia! This castle is a deathtrap. We should have prepared our defenses and faced the dragon when he came to Avejion.*

The castle is a deathtrap. But whose death it will claim remains to be determined. This is the first time I have faced ogres, but I have fought many times with dragons over the centuries. One thing I have learned, you do not want to face them on an open battlefield. NO DEFENSES have ever proven strong enough. Here, in his den, he feels powerful; unbeatable; supreme. That will be his undoing.

CHAPTER 7

STORM OF FIRE

Apollonia entered the castle as Napoli's men regrouped. "Where are my brothers?" demanded Jacques. He was aware they disappeared into the bowels and figured Apollonia had sent them on a mission.

"They are in search of Rooskie, the last of Shabodun's protectors." Apollonia began to leave the men in the hall then turned back, "you must reach Shabodun's lair before the sun rises. He may fight you now, but come the sunrise, he will destroy you all. It is time to bring in the chains and the rest of the powder kegs. Remember the bridge, be extremely careful around these torches."

The men rolled the wagons in and informed Napoli the other witches were gone. He told them Apollonia had disappeared into the castle as well. They were on their own once again. He didn't like the way Apollonia and her daughters had misled them. He had counted on her help in this fight but except for the battle on the bridge, it had been him and his men that faced these horrors. Paul came out of a dark corridor with an urgency that could only mean he had found the last ogre.

"Yes," he told them. "Several levels below this hall, is one just as large. He sits in front of a stone door; it is the only door in the room. The dragon must be sleeping there."

"Then let's be done with this unholy task quickly," Napoli told the others.

They followed Paul's directions down winding narrow stone steps. The passage was tight; they had to make their way in single file with their backs against the wall. Somewhere within the narrow corridor they had to stop and pass the weapons down one at a time. The walls were smooth like those in the cave, no cracks or markings from a tool could be felt. Jacques didn't like this; it felt like a trap. "Are you sure there is no other way?"

"This is the only way I can remember."

Maybe it was the way he answered, or the sound of his voice, but Jacques didn't like what he heard. "Quickly, everyone, back up the passage." He ordered. "We got to get out of here, now!"

Paul was still heading in the wrong direction. He was descending as the others were trying to get past him. Jacques tackled the boy and allowed the others to use his back as a steppingstone. He was about to get up and pull Paul to his feet when he felt the air rush past his face. He yelled, "Take cover!"

The narrow corridor filled with heat and a bright yellow glow reflected off the glass-like walls. A ball of fire rolled upward from far below. His hair singed and his back burnt. Pain, brief but intense, paralyzed him. Above him were the screams of those who were caught standing and took the full brunt of the fireball. His brother was safe beneath him for the moment, but they needed to get out of there. They raced up the steps. They tripped over two of their friends who had perished in the dragon's attack. Their bodies were charred to a black and rock-like form which crumbled as they landed on them. Who of their friends had perished was unidentifiable and unknowable in the moment.

"I'm sorry, brother," Paul said, "I didn't know what I was doing. My thoughts were not from my head. I tried but I could not stop being pulled in here."

"I know." Jacques sympathized, "Don't worry about that, we just need to find the opening."

Hands grabbed the two and pulled them from the corridor just as another fireball rolled up. The men had found another room halfway up the passage. The dragon, Shabodun, could be heard moving through the castle. The walls vibrated from the slapping of his tail. The sounds echoing all around them like funeral drums. The men didn't know it, but Shabodun was using the beating of his tail to locate the intruders, much like a bat locates its prey.

The men had been separated in four small groups and Shabodun was moving in on Jacques and his brother. Without weapons to defend themselves, Jacques ordered them back to the main hall. Their only problem was finding steps that would lead them there. The castle's lower region was a labyrinth, a multitude of passages and stairs, some that led to dead ends.

They ran from one huge room to the next, found a stairway and listened to the sounds of the dragon breathing. When it was quiet, they ran to the next level. They no sooner cleared a passage before the heat of the dragon's fire would race up behind them. Shabodun was hunting Jacques and Paul.

"I can feel his eyes upon me," Paul said in dismay. His face twisted and his body trembled uncontrollably with fear.

"I feel him too," Jacques wrapped his arms around his little brother. He felt the power of the dragon's mind and knew the grip it had on his brother. "But we are here together. Clear your mind of all thoughts and just follow me."

Jacques followed a calling in his mind. A familiar voice whispered, "turn left… go this way." After several close calls, they reached the main hall. Apollonia was waiting for them, "You must all stay together now. Use the chains to hold Shabodun in place and ignite the powder to destroy him."

"There is a flaw in your plan, isn't there?" demanded

Jacques, anger rising in his voice. "You don't know if the powder will kill him."

"To the best of my knowledge, it is the only way to kill him," admitted Apollonia. "This powder comes all the way from the Eastern Edge. It is said to be able to rip a dragon apart."

"And if you are wrong?" questioned Paul, his eyes locked on his feet unable to bear the gaze of his companions. "Or if there is not enough powder."

"Then we all perish here."

As the men began to argue with each other, she slipped out of their sight again.

It wasn't long before Rooskie made himself known. He was smaller than the previous ogres and shorter too, if ten feet and three-hundred pounds could be considered short and light. His body was covered in black spikes six inches long. He disappeared in the shadows. The men had very few weapons left.

Then Paul exclaimed, "I have an idea!"

R ooskie looked around the main hall at the men who were taking shelter behind the columns. He walked over to his fallen brother and stuck a finger in the hole in Hammolt's neck.

"Very clever for men, are you. Hammolt was simple and Dool was even a lesser creature. You will find I am not so easily overcome by your tricks."

Napoli was amazed that the ogre could speak. He thought of them as mindless beasts acting on primal impulses. "If you are as smart as you think you are, then you know we are not here for you. We have come for your master. We came for Shabodun. Leave us to him and we will leave you with your life."

"That is generous and forgiving of you," Rooskie smiled, "especially considering I feasted on your father, and left his bones for dust. I wonder if the son has the same flavor. You carry his scent. I never forget a smell."

Napoli charged at the ogre and Peter tackled him just shy of one of his spiked hairs. He pulled his brother back to safety. "He is trying to bait you into an attack. He seeks to divide us. We must take him together. We will keep him distracted while Paul and the others prepare the trap. If he killed our father, he will pay dearly for it."

Napoli nodded then watched his brother, and ten others slip into passages behind the ogre. They went up the narrow passages, appearing thirty feet above the hall. Paul waved, signaling his brothers to back the ogre into position.

"Your brothers were much more formidable than you. They put up quite a fight. I think we will just poke out your eyes and leave you to wander in darkness." Napoli taunted the giant. "You are not worth our time to kill." He took a spear and carefully approached, making fake throwing motions, forcing the ogre to back up. The others took up the spears and swords and surrounded the ogre. Now, they had no fear, the true danger was who the ogre protected below them. Still, they approached cautiously.

Rooskie slashed at the men using the spikes on his arms as weapons. A single brush of his razor-sharp hair was enough to cut a man in two. Swords shattered against the thick course bristles that covered his arms and legs. Their shields were wooden but covered with iron plates and straps. They absorbed the blows and remained intact. Rooskie's skin was softer than his brothers' hide, and the spears penetrated it causing him to howl and retreat.

Napoli called out, "This one is soft! Crossbows and arrows, men, we will take him at a distance."

The beast charged forward and slashed wildly at the men. He was quicker than the other ogres, knocking them to the ground with each attack. However, before he could strike a killing blow, the other half of the men charged in and inflicted wounds of their own. Napoli pulled Merci from its buckskin bow sleeve in the wagon, within seconds strung it and let fly a deadly black obsidian arrowhead. It struck deep into Rooskie's arm. Two others fired bolts from their crossbows, hitting his left side and the right thigh above the knee. They had him in a crossfire and unleashed a fierce barrage of arrows, spears, and sword strikes. Their battle plan was working; they flanked him on two fronts and gave him little chance to defend himself.

Napoli and his men backed Rooskie to the wall. Paul dropped a chain down over his head and around his neck. Stones tumbled from out of openings above, tightening the noose around the ogre's neck. Rooskie was lifted off his feet and squirmed for air.

Napoli yelled up, "I will still spare your life and just take your black eyes if you tell me how to find your master, Shabodun."

"Look to the sun. He is the blackness within. My life as a servant is over. Your pain is just starting."

If anyone thought Rooskie was conceding his defeat, they were wrong. He was making a bold prediction, a prophecy he fully expected to see fulfilled in the coming moments. Rooskie calmed himself. Black blood and green bile flowed down his body in rivulets from the arrows and spears stuck in his flesh. He took deep breaths. The chains around his neck expanded and contracted as he did. He stared out of the two great holes in the mountain that formed the eyes in the face of the castle. The sun was rising over the top of the mountain, and those orbs began to brighten. Rooskie smiled.

There appeared a great shadow that moved slowly across the main hall of the castle. The men ducked into whatever passage or cranny they could find. The dragon's body blotted out the morning sun. Napoli managed a solitary glimpse before Shabodun's mouth filled with crimson slurry and hurled a fireball their way. It broke against the mountain's face and the flames flooded the main hall, turning the walls red hot. The air seized everything in the hall, shields, spears, swords then ripped them out in a tumultuous explosion. Melted rock ran like water down the outside of the mountain's face.

Rooskie sucked in the flames, allowing the glowing mass to rupture his body. In the haze of heat and fire, he cried out in anguish and pain. But it was not a sound of misery. It was the joyful screams of birth. His body twisted and broke free of the chains. When he dropped to the ground the mountain shook. He had grown twice his size and tripled in weight in seconds. His arms and legs stretched out, fingers and toes transforming into thickening claws. A deep red glow filled his eye sockets. His chest heaved and glowed fiendishly.

Finish him now or you will never leave this mountain alive.

Napoli heeded Apollonia's command and charged the beast with an iron spike in hand. Both hands holding it at waist level. He did not stop. He did not slow his attack. He ran headlong driving the spike through the eye of Rooskie and into his brain. He slowly pulled himself from the skull of the monster that lay in mid-transformation, part ogre, part dragon. His head had doubled in size, capable of swallowing Jacques' body whole. His teeth were double rows of jagged knives. The inside row pointing out and the outside row pointing in. They formed a scissor pattern that with the top rows would have shredded its foes. Wings had sprouted but withered on his back. His body was still fat and stubby as an ogre's but tripled in size. Jacques was drenched in the monster's fluids, no longer black or green, a bright orange which burned like pepper. He had slain Rooskie just in time.

The dragon flew off. The men watched, knowing exactly where he was heading. He soared high in the sky, casting his shadow over the land. The strange cloud raced over the fields of brown furrows and parched green sprouts. The walls of the city were a mere line of dots on the landscape to Shabodun. The gathering of stone and wooden houses made a point for him to unleash his tirade.

How dare you come to my home and challenge my power. I will show you fools what it means to defy a dragon. I will teach you, Jacques Napoli, the folly of joining forces with the sea witches and their kind.

His words burned in their minds. Shabodun dove out of the sun. The people of the town wouldn't see him coming. He was a black spot in the otherwise bright yellow sunshine. A hundred feet above the guard towers he opened his mouth and filled himself to near bursting. His chest expanded and swelled. Heat built up inside of him causing a great flush of pain, his eyes closed, fighting back the loss of consciousness. As he crossed the city wall, only inches from the tower roof, the dragon roared.

A torrent of fire filled the streets of Avejion. Houses of stone and wood erupted and exploded from the force thrown against them. A sea of flames spread in all directions consuming everything in its path. Shabodun flapped once and rose back toward the heavens. He circled and dove again at the city in flames, determined to leave nothing behind but black burnt earth.

The second fireball, greater than the first, hit what was moments ago, the center of the town. It lifted everything that was Avejion high into the air and scattered it as tiny glowing embers. Shabodun landed with an earth-quaking thud. He looked around, not even the walls of the city stood before him.

He stomped in triumph and glee. *See what following the Sea Witch brings. Apollonia, I still hunger for your flesh. Stop hiding among these foolish men. Give yourself to me and I will relieve you of your pain. Surely, you tire of this life.*

J acques Napoli and his men were overcome with grief. They stood in shocked horror feeling the dragon's taunts. Witnessing the devastation through his eyes. In the distance the black cloud rose like a thin satin funeral ribbon floating in the air from what had once been their homes. Their families, gone. Their lives, ruined. But if Shabodun had thought to break these men, he had miscalculated his actions. His fire did not destroy them. He galvanized their spirit. Turned their will from iron to steel. Each in his own heart vowing not to leave the mountain while the dragon, Shabodun, still drew breath.

Apollonia returned to the group. They were transfixed. She loaded one of the wagons with iron cages as they stared off towards their homeland.

Napoli became aware of her presence as she tied down the wagon's tarp. "What is that you have there?"

Apollonia was reluctant to answer, but the others' eyes burned with hatred. "They are called Molytans. They are prisoners of the dragon; we must get them away from here before he returns."

Jacques swung his sword, cutting the lines and sending the tarp flying. Ten square cages, four feet on each side, were neatly stored on the wagon that had carried the irons. Inside the cages were delicate childlike beings whose skin glowed like dull gold. There was a great despondency about them, and it weighted on each man's heart. "Is this why you brought us here? Is this why my friends and families died? To free these… these… spirits of yours."

"You came to this mountain to kill a dragon and save your loved ones. I told you to get it done before dawn," Apollonia said callously, "You did not."

Aberash shot a stern look past Jacques at Apollonia. *Mother, you are too harsh on this man. Surely, we should ease his pain.*

He is angry, which is good and bad, but we need him focused. He is no good to anyone if he is blinded by the dragon.

And Shabodun has easy access to these men now. We must be on guard against that weakness.

Jacques could faintly hear the maidens' thoughts even though not directed towards him. He felt there was a dishonesty between them. It was a feeling he held since first meeting Apollonia. She revealed much but also held much back. Once he joined their triad it was harder to keep him out of their communications. He swung the sword at her, stopping inches from her throat. "Well, at least you got what you came for. I suppose you and your daughters will transform into horses and run away."

"Don't be a fool, Jacques! This battle is far from over. Do you think Shabodun will let you be? You still have a dragon to kill."

"Why? What have we left to fight for?" Jacques dropped his sword, and its clamor filled the empty chamber. "Let the dragon have his mountain."

No one in the main hall moved an inch. Their fingers tightened on the weapons in hand. They were just as hurt and bitter as he was. He knew he could not leave the mountain, for whatever reason Apollonia needed to rescue these creatures, his mission was still the same, to kill the dragon on the mountain. He meekly picked up his sword.

CHAPTER 8
LIVE EVIL

"This is my mission," admitted Apollonia. "I have tracked this dragon for centuries as he rounded up the Molytans for himself. They are part of his source of power. They are essential to stop the rise and spread of more dragons in this world. Your mission remains the same, you must destroy or capture the dragon here. Shabodun will do everything in his power to keep these Molytans under his control. They are his prisoners."

"Why are they so important to the dragon?" Paul asked.

"Dragons are neither born nor die. They transform from the Molytan to the ogre and finally to the dragon. One dragon controls the transformation of another. Shabodun was transformed by Deyhezas. Napoli stopped him from transforming Rooskie into a dragon. With these ten Molytans at his disposal, he can create more ogres or dragons as he wishes. And they are also essential to healing his wounds. He uses their life force to enhance and regenerate his body. Without the Molytans it would take decades for him to recover from a battle."

Jack, a childhood friend of Jacques, stepped forward from the men who remained. He had been on the steps when five of his friends were incinerated. Jack escaped death when he tripped running up the steps as the fireball raced inches above him. He watched the bodies of his friends turn to ash and bones. The dragon's flame blowing the flesh off them in a flash. Hate swelled within him. He said, "So, they are likened to his family. This Shabodun has taken our friends and family, it is time we show him the same. Let him feel the pain he has caused us. If they be the source of dragons and their power, I see but one solution." He drew his sword saying, "We end this reign of terror here and now."

"Noooo!" Apollonia grabbed the sword's blade as Jack thrusted it towards the cage. It sliced through her hand; the tip pierced the Molytan's chest. A flash of light brighter than the noonday sun radiated from the tiny slit in the creature. Apollonia's hand healed instantly, not losing a drop of blood. Jack was not so fortunate.

One half of his face, the side facing the Molytan he attacked, sizzled, smoke arid and rancid rising from it. The right side of Jack's face turned apple-red, then black. His eye turned marble-white and motionless. Everywhere the light fell on him, burning from his arm to his face, was scarred and deformed. Intense and excruciating pain coursed through his body as if his blood had turned to a river of fire. Jack dropped the sword, its tip melted and dulled. He fell to the floor in convulsions.

Avia ran to him. She cradled his head in her lap and stroked the side of his face. She held emeralds, bloodstone, amethysts, shards of citrine, clear quartz, sapphires and turquoise in her left hand. They glowed and she sang as he shook from the pain. Jack was going into shock, but he would be dead already if she had not acted and absorbed the massive amount of energy that struck him. The stones allowed her to store the excessive forces her young body could not contain. They channeled their healing powers through her into him. He was lucky Apollonia had stopped the blade from creating a larger gash and releasing a greater amount of the Molytan's lifeforce. If he had been successful, all of them would have been burned to ashes.

The Molytan's body glowed brightly and the others began to shimmer in response. A great rush of wind filled the castle with a cry of anger. It was a sound that came from far away.

Apollonia looked each man in the eye and gave a stern warning, "The Molytans cannot be harmed. They are not your enemy. They are no danger to anyone. They serve a purpose in this world as old as life. It is their power which keeps the world in balance. When disease, death, and decay spread, or threatens to overtake the healthy, it is the Molytans who come and with their fire burn it away. The dragons have taken their purpose and corrupted it. They have become the very thing the Molytans are meant to destroy. It is the dragons that are now death and destruction in this world. They crave death above all else." She turned sullen; the years showing through her expression as if age had suddenly befallen her. "The Molytans cannot transform themselves into dragons. They cannot transform another Molytan into a dragon either. Nor do they desire to become one themselves. The Molytans do not wish to serve the dragons. But their lifeforce is symbiotic with the dragons. And now, Shabodun knows we have them, he returns for them."

"If he comes for them then they shall be his downfall," announced Jacques. "He killed our families; we will kill him when he comes for his." Jacques led the men down into the castle. They took the iron chains, spikes, and shackles deep inside. They took the remaining kegs of black powder too.

They set their trap below the second great hall. The huge archways of the hall formed the mouth of the face in the mountain; it was how the dragon entered the castle. The dragon's hide was much too thick to attack with spears or swords. Peter and Paul had set up a system of weights and pulleys to shackle the dragon, much in the same way as they had done to Rooskie. But this was a dragon, a hundred times stronger than an ogre. They would need to use spikes to pin the dragon down.

Apollonia and the twins descended into the lower catacombs of the mountain castle. She had the men carry the cages deep into the mountain and told them, "Shabodun will follow like a dog tracking a rabbit. Retrieving the Molytans will blind him to everything else. He will not be able to focus on you like he did before but your thoughts may still be known to him collectively. Try not to think about what you must do, just act when the time is right."

They set their trap in a tight narrowing tunnel not wide enough for the dragon to crawl in as he was. They worked quickly, driving the spikes through the ends of the chains. Shabodun would have to crawl through the tunnel, he would step into the shackles. His weight was enough to pull the chains taunt and drive other spikes into his neck behind his head. The place where Apollonia said the dragon's armor plating was the thinnest. The plan was to use the dragon's own power against him. It was a bold plan with many possibilities for failure. The chains might not hold him. He could use his massive body and strength to cause a cave in, burying all of them alive. She told them keeping the Molytans close to them would prevent him from such an attack. It provided little comfort to them.

J ack was not so sure the twins' plan would work. What if Shabodun realized it was a trap? He could see into their minds, just as the witch had been doing. What if the chains didn't hold him? And for how long must they trap him there for the dragon to die? What if the black powder was not enough to kill him? These things troubled Jack and he pulled Jacques aside. "We must have a second plan."

"In case the twins fail."

"Yes and no. We need a plan to assure the dragon never leaves this mountain," he said. "In case chains and spikes are not enough. And even if they are, we want to be sure we rid the world of this thing forever."

"And you have such a plan?"

"I do. And the fewer who know it, the least likely the dragon will discover it." Jack took hold of Jacques' arm and gave it a reaffirming squeeze. "You know how he led us into a trap before; we must be on our guard that he does not turn us against ourselves."

"This be the truth," agreed Jacques. "It has been hard to know which thoughts are our own this day, and which have been planted, or by whom. How many will you need?"

"Just you," he smiled, "and a few others." Then he led six of the men quietly from the lower hall.

S habodun flew into the lower hall, flapped his wings and caused a howling hurricane that raced throughout the castle. The men in all parts of the castle were blown off their feet. Some were slammed into walls or sent tumbling down the stairs by the sudden gust of wind. He kept up the onslaught of air until he could smell where everyone was to be found. Their scent carried back to him on the wild wind currents.

He was especially pleased to locate the warm fragrance of his Molytans. He smiled with delight, knowing they were taken deeper into the mountain. The sea witches had made a grand misjudgment. Trying to escape through the bowels of his castle was a fool's goal. It was a maze of deathtraps he built. No escape was possible. It was a thousand feet straight down from where they were hiding. And her companions, which laid in wait for him with chains and iron would not stop him from reclaiming what was his. And at long last he would claim her life too.

The rest of the men were trying to escape above, and he would deal with them soon enough. Shabodun slithered through the larger tunnels down into the mountain.

Did you really think you could escape me? I know every inch of this mountain. I have been carving out my home here since I fought that old fool Vargrerot. Sea witch, you thought I went limping back to Deyhezas. No, I have been building my own kingdom in the mountain. I control these mountains. I know these mountains. I will make them your graveyard.

How many times have you claimed my life now? And how many times have you failed? Now, I have your precious Moly-tans. Now I hold the source of your power. Without them you will wither and die. You shall dry up like old rotten fruit. And I shall sit here and watch.

No man nor sea witch has ever taken the life of a dragon. Although, countless have tried. As you yourself can attest to.

Well, today shall be a special day in your life. You shall be the first of your kind to give up his life. I can assure you; you will not be the last to lose his life to man and maiden.

A roar and burst of heat rumbled through the mountain.

Peter shook with fear. Suddenly, sitting in the dark cramp confines of the tunnel, this plan didn't seem such a good idea.

Apollonia squeezed his hand, "he is just shedding energy, making himself skinnier so he can fit into the smaller tunnels. This is what we want, as he shrinks, he will be weaker when he gets down to us. His fire less of a weapon to use against us. Have faith."

Peter nodded but was not any more confident they made the right choice. A small dragon was still a dragon. But they could not flee now. There was the edge of the cliff behind them and the dragon somewhere in the dark before them. If he made it around the bend without triggering the trap, then it was either a fall to their death or be burned and eaten. There was no way out without victory. He could hear the scraping of Shabodun's claws as he made his way towards them. His roars, louder. His fire, hotter. His body, weaker.

Paul sat motionless in a nook by the first set of shackles. He had to wait for the dragon's fore legs to pass before positioning them in place for its hind legs. He felt this to be his duty and redemption for getting so many killed earlier. He shut out all thoughts. The closer the dragon came, the stronger he felt its pull on his mind. He was searching for them by sight, smell, sound, and thought. His mind was the most powerful weapon he wielded. Fear weakened the men and exposed them to Shabodun. Paul was strong as the stone that hid him from view as Shabodun's claws thundered past him.

As weak as he was, he was still massive and formidable. His eye was larger than Paul's body, but he did not look his way. Teeth the size of Paul's arm dripped puddles of saliva as he walked. Paul had never seen the dragon; his image had been implanted in his mind when Shabodun took control of him. It was an incomplete, fuzzy, out of focus image like a nightmare. Physically, he was terrifying.

Paul tugged the rope. It ran dangerously close to the belly of the dragon. He wasn't sure if Shabodun would feel it if it brushed against him. He had to pull it slow and steady as not to rattle the chains. The two shackles slid into place just as Shabodun's hind leg landed in one. His weight caused the smaller chains that formed a netting to slip through the larger link of the leg ring, tightening it.

Shabodun shook his leg. *Ah, Paul, you have found your*

courage. That is good. It will make killing you more enjoyable. He tried to turn, and his other hind leg got tangled in the snare. He thrashed about trying to cause a cave in, but all the rocks fell on him. He leaped forward, and both his front claws landed and were trapped in the chains. Shabodun stabbed at the walls with his tail, trying in vain to impale Paul. The crusted, boney tip pounding holes in the rock.

Paul slipped down a tiny duct behind him, his part of the plan a success.

These chains will never hold me.

But they did and as he pulled and struggled the iron spikes swung down from another corridor, striking behind his ears. Large boulders helped to drive them into place. He tried to roar but the eight spikes locked his jaws shut. The pain infuriated Shabodun as much as the humiliation of the trap. Unable to open his mouth fully he blew fire from his nostrils. Small and weak was the flame he produced.

The flames he exhaled in anger worked against him. He was hoping to escape the trap by melting his bindings. But he couldn't turn his head completely around and his fire was becoming weaker. As he lost power in the darkness he continued to shrink, and the chains tightened even more. The spikes burrowed deeper into his head.

Apollonia wished they would sever it completely. Part of the dragon's trap was the unfurling of a chain down the shaft behind her and the men. They used the dragon's weight to anchor one end of the chain and lowered themselves to the floor.

There were passages at the bottom of the shaft that led through the mountain to the outside, to find the right one would take some time.

Peter said, "where is Jacques and the others?"

Paul looked around and realized they were not part of the group. "I haven't seen them since we started down the tunnels. I guess I thought they were with you."

Apollonia said, "they are still above. We must move quickly from here."

"Why?"

"Where?"

"It doesn't matter," she told the twins. "They have a plan of their own and we can't be here."

Jacques and Jack could feel the heat rising in one of the stairwells. They heard the dragon's pitiful moans and weak roar. The twin's trap had worked. They had driven four spikes into opposite walls of the castle's main hall. The six men snaked the heaviest chains down and around pillars along the outer walls. They placed the kegs of black powder in small rooms below where the spikes anchored the chains.

While the six men worked on their plan, Jack led Jacques down a twisting stone stairway. He had scouted out another way down the castle that took them behind the dragon. At the end of the steps there was a great conduit that appeared as smooth as glass. Jack tossed in a torch. It slid for a long time down and around the bends, its light becoming dim but never completely going dark.

"What is this place?"

"I'm not sure. I don't know where it leads but it goes far below the castle."

"How do you know of…"

"I became aware of it when I stabbed the Molytan," Jack admitted knowing what his friend was thinking.

Jacques looked down the hole again then back to Jack. "This could be a trap. The dragon's control over you."

"I thought that myself," Jack confessed, "but this whole plan of mine came to me in that moment of pain. I think it was the Molytan. I think they want me to do this. To free them from their dragon master, they showed me how to destroy him and escape."

Jacques studied his friend carefully. He didn't have the same vagueness of spirit that his brother had exhibited earlier. They had gone too far to turn back; he trusted Jack was right.

Jack found the oils that covered the men while digging. He positioned barrels on the steps leading to the twins' dragon snare. They poured barrels of oil across the main hall and down into the rooms with black powder. Jack hoped Shabodun wouldn't come in breathing fire or all would be for naught. They needed him to wait until the trap was sprung and then he could light up the place. They pulled the ropes and tipped the barrels over and ran as fast as they could to outrun the oil.

A small black river flowed down through the maze of tunnels and stairwells. It ran thick and slow, oozing its way to the dragon in the dark. The volatile liquid creeped before Shabodun's face. He did not see it in the dark tunnel. That is, until he exhaled and set the oil ablaze. He struggled frantically against the chains tightening their grip and driving the spikes deeper. He knew the flames would be the last part of the men's plan. He needed to escape now, but the chains would not give way. He had never felt iron as strong as these bindings. He tried inhaling the flames for strength, but it was of no use, they weren't hot enough. He had weakened himself too much in his pursuit of the Sea Witch.

The castle glowed brightly. The eyes burned a deep orange. The mouth blenched a cloud of yellow flame. The mountain smoked. Then thunder ripped the mountain apart. Humongous boulders blasted from the face in four different places. Gigantic slabs of rock folded from the castle's facade.

The mountain quaked, and the men tumbled down the stone steps. The noise was so loud no one could hear anything. The four walls blew out and crumbled from the blast of black powder. The spikes anchored in those walls were ejected into the air with the chains behind them. The chains snapped tight from the weight of the stones cascading down the mountainside. They popped the stone columns supporting the main hall ceiling like dried timber. The ceiling could no longer hold the mountain's peak aloft. It was the sound of the castle caving in that overpowered all hearing. Tons of rocks poured into the caverns of the mountain castle filling every open space. The weight crushed down the mountain peak, compacting it back to solid rock.

Air rushing into the tunnels both forced Jack, Jacques, and the six down their escape route and cushioned their landing at the bottom. They found themselves in total darkness buried in sand and rubble deep within the mountain.

The mountain had been transformed once again. This time in a matter of minutes rather than the years, decades, and centuries Shabodun had taken. Jacques, his band of fifty men, three witches from the sea, and their black powder from the East had done the impossible. The collapsing castle buried Shabodun inside his mountain.

CHAPTER 9

LIFE IN DARKNESS

Jacques, Jack, and the six others found a shallow river inside a cave. At first it was nothing more than a slick streak on the tunnel floor. But that turned into a few inches of water trickling down through the cave. They followed it knowing that water ran downhill and soon it was up to their calves. The others, led by Apollonia, soon found them. Luck and Apollonia were on their side, the water led her to them. The mountain had changed. Jack's plan drastically morphed the mountain's topography. Other than a few small caves and mines that cut through the mountain, no one had any idea what was to be found inside. They were still trapped in the darkness, but they made it deep enough in the mountain that they were safe from the falling rocks. Finding a way out would not be easy.

Jacques Napoli told them, "We may have to dig our way out." He feared with all their supplies gone they wouldn't last long inside the mountain.

They were following the water which was flowing freely and hopeful that it was running out of the mountain somewhere and not pooling some place in the darkness. They lit only one torch to conserve, not the torches, but the air. Some of the tunnels were sparkling multicolored fissures, twisting and hard to navigate, their walls sharp as swords to the touch. These were natural crystalline formations in the mountain, some undoubtedly ripped open by the explosions and cave ins. Other openings were the results of mining operations that took place over the centuries.

The mountain provided for people above and below its surface. Some of the caves led to abysses, and more than once they had to turn back from the edge of a cliff as the water disappeared into the darkness. There was no sound of a splash in the black holes. So, they doubled back and picked up another tributary running off into the unknown. Then there were tunnels of smooth glass, like the one Jacques and his friends used to escape the blast. These were round tubular dragon-made structures, dead ends created as traps, or perhaps a place to hide.

The mountain had not finished morphing either. Every few hours it rumbled and groaned; Jacques worried how much damage had they caused. He also feared that despite their best efforts, they had failed to kill Shabodun, and he was digging his way towards them. But the earthquakes didn't seem to bother Apollonia, or her daughters, so he kept his concerns to himself. They kept following the water down the mountain.

Jacques came upon the twins one day; they had broken a shield into pieces and were tossing the parts on a flat rock. "What are you two doing?"

"Playing a game," answered Paul.

"Why not? We have been searching for days, down one tunnel, up another. One dead end after another. We are taking a break. We made these placards to remember our victory over the dragon." Peter handed his older brother the wooden chips. One had a crude likeness of Jacques. The others, now only twenty-two in number, gathered around the dimly lit rock.

"Is this me?" Jacques held up the one with his face wearing a crown.

"Yes," said Paul and smiled. "You are the King of Spears.

Can you tell who this one is?" He held up another of the small wooden squares.

Jack grabbed it from his hand angrily. It had a drawing of him with half his face and one eye missing. "Very funny."

"I call it the One Eye Jack." Paul laughed heartily. "And this one is Viola, she is your Queen, Jacques."

Jacques' heart sank. He had not thought of his wife and family since the battle's end. He took a little comfort in that he saw no one on the streets of Avejion when Shabodun attacked. He consoled himself thinking they died in their sleep instantly and unaware of what happened. Now here she was. His brothers painted a great likeness of her from the many minerals around them. Her yellow hair flowing down the blue smock she often wore.

"I didn't mean to upset you," Paul said when he saw the tears forming in his brother's eyes.

"It's just the smoke," Jacques lied and quickly swiped the back of his hand across his face. The battle with the dragon had cost them everything. Their families were gone, their homes destroyed, and now they were probably going to die buried in the same tomb as the dragon. But his brothers seemed to find levity in their situation, most likely because of their young age. "So, how do you two fools play this game?"

Peter took the placards, placed them face down and mixed them around. Each brother took half and one at a time turned a placard over. There were numbers and symbols on each. "Seven of Spears against the Five of Arrows, I win," announced Peter grabbing the wooden chips. They turned over another placard.

"Eight of Clubs against his Three of Swords. I win," said Paul and collected the cards from the rock. Next, they turned over Jacques' card and one that resembled his friend Pierre, the King of Arrows. "It's a tie, so now we must fight. I… Declare… War." The two brothers turned over a card with each word.

Paul's last card was a Ten of Swords. Peter turned over Apollonia's card, the Queen of Swords.

"I win," Peter exclaimed and swept all the cards to his side of the table.

"And what do you call this game?"

Peter looked up at his brother as if he should have known. "War, of course."

"There are fifty cards representing us and two cards that represent the dragons, the most powerful cards," Paul said.

"The most powerful?" Questioned Jacques. "That doesn't seem right. We defeated the dragon, did we not? And there was but one, not two."

"Ah, but there would have been two if not for the swift and strong King of Spears," explained Paul. "And the dragons are the most powerful cards, able to defeat any one man here. It was the might of fifty that won. And this is a two-man game, so we need to have an even number of pieces."

"Interesting," said Apollonia as she transformed from a large serpent back into a woman. She no longer hid her powers from the men.

Their brief contact with her and her daughters enlightened the men to their true nature. They knew it was by their power that they were able to defeat Shabodun and his ogres. Although she was much larger than the actual animal, they were amazed at how small her body could become. Each transformation weakened her and the other maidens. She could manage bats, rats, and cats, but nothing larger. Not the giant bear that did battle for them.

"I have found a way out of the caves." She told them. "We will have to move some large boulders, the explosions caused massive landslides. Where there was once a cave opening is now blocked, but your brothers are quite clever and should be able to devise a way."

Jacques carried one of the cages as they followed Apollonia.

The Molytan Jack had stabbed had dimmed again, his iridescence fading. Jacques looked at the others, they all seemed to be dying. They lay motionless in the cages. Their breath was slow and shallow. Their eyes, once bright blue as the summer skies, were black pools of a starless night. He realized four weeks had passed. He kept time by tying a knot in a rope every time a new torch was lit. Each oil-soaked torch burned for a day.

When they first regrouped and took stock of the supplies they had, food was the least in quantity. Rationing the bread to a quarter of a loaf a man, it was finished in ten days. However, no one was hungry or even thought of food.

The Molytans provided sustenance to the dragons and now to us. Their energy will not last for much longer with so many of us feeding from them. We must get them out of the darkness before they die, and we with them. They need the energy of the sun. They feed on the light.

We should build a fire. Let them regain their strength before it is too late.

That is very noble, Jacques. But a fire will not do, it is not the same as sunlight. We cannot build a fire hot enough to provide the energy they absorb from the sun. We must get them out of this mountain.

What will become of them? Jacques was getting the hang of mind speak, he could direct his thought to Apollonia. And he was able to see clearly the images behind her thoughts.

My sisters and I will take them to an island far out of reach of any dragons. We have made our home across the ocean. Dragons cannot fly that far, nor can they swim. They will not attempt to cross the ice at the top of the world; it would take too much fire to keep from freezing in the barren artic wilderness. They will be safe with us. We will tend to the Molytans and release them after all the dragons are vanquished. I must warn you, Jacques, once we exit the mountains, the other dragons will sense their life energy, they will come for them, and you.

Why me?

"You are now known as Napoleon, the Dragon Slayer," she announced loudly. She wanted all the men to be part of this conversation. "There are other dragons, in particular, one to the north in the British Isles and another to the east beyond these mountains. When you leave here, you must take stones from this mountain and build a castle around your homeland. Others will flock to you, now that they know of your deeds. Some will come to aid you; others will be sent to destroy you."

"Why, Apollonia? Killing a dragon is a good thing," Paul remarked.

"Not to other dragons, lad." Apollonia pointed to a rubble mound blocking their way. It was the way out, but most of the rocks were man-size at the least. "Dragons have long fought for control and just for the sake of blood. But when someone like Jacques finds a way to defeat one of their kind, they will do anything to keep that knowledge from spreading. You see, Shabodun is not dead, but has been turned into his Ruby Cradle. Asleep so to speak, only another dragon, or a Molytan can free him. Jacques, when you build your castle, you will encase the Ruby Cradle in an iron box and keep it deep within the walls of your castle. The other dragons will come for it and you, you must end their reign."

"If I did not slay the dragon then why am I being called Napoleon," Jacques was uneasy with claiming a false victory. "Why not tell the truth about what happened here?"

"Would you rather be known as Jacques Napoli, the man who dropped a mountain on a dragon, that will one day return to ravish your lands and kill your people… It doesn't inspire people to your side and is quite lengthy for a coat of arms, don't you think?"

"You speak of people already knowing of our deeds. How could they? We have barely come to realized what we have done here."

"You knew your friend, Pierre, was in trouble. How?"

"I don't know," he said, ashamed of his lacking a true understanding of the conversation he was having. "It was just a feeling I had. In my gut or in the back of my mind that would not let me rest."

"Yes," Apollonia validated his statement and smiled, "it is a power that is shared among all living creatures. It knows no boundaries. Birds know birds and men know men. And some, like mermaids and dragons, can know both, and many more. So, yes, your deeds will be known, by men, mermaids, and dragons. You, all of you, must be ready for what that knowledge will bring. Your war is not over. It has not been won. There will be more battles to be fought, more dragons to defeat. But hence forth, you will never fight alone."

The twins built a swing that hoisted a large boulder and slammed it against the rubble. The boulder struck with deafening repercussions inside the cave. The men worked in teams of five pulling the rock to its highest point then letting it slam into the rock wall. It sent fragments flying from the barricade. The rest retreated far up the tunnel and cupped their hands over their ears. It was little protection from the hammering at the cave's entrance. The cave was old and solidly formed and Apollonia guaranteed that a collapse was impossible. More importantly, shock waves in the rock caused a dull thudding drumbeat heard outside the cave.

The sound drew the attention of those who wandered aimlessly on the mountainside, still caught in the fog of the dragon's possession. For those who spent years and decades under its influence a sudden release was nearly impossible. The explosions and landslides caught many off guard. Hundreds were killed in a matter of moments as the mountain swept them away in a sea of rocks and dirt. Mercifully, they had no idea what was happening to them, still trapped within the dragon's clutches, the crushing blow went unheeded.

In such cataclysmic events, death never was achieved in totality. Whether it was pure luck or divine providence many survived the avalanche, both above the rocks and debris, and below. Now, the sound of the men in the mountain brought those who were in search of lost loved ones up the mountain again. Pierre and his men found the place where Jacques was trapped. They used sledgehammers and iron bars to remove the rockslide from the cave's mouth. It took weeks to cause enough of the rubble to fall and provide an opening suitable for the men to pass through. They were overjoyed to see daylight and the rivers flowing down the mountains once again. Jacques was happiest to see his old friend freed from the curse of Shabodun.

"It was like a nightmare you cannot awake from," Pierre confided. "The horrible things we did. We tried to resist, but his command was compelling, his voice drowned out all other thoughts. And then there was the burning. Every second of every day, I was burned from the inside out. The pain was unbearable and unending. There was no fighting it. No rest from the dragon's will. I was in Hell."

Jacques had no words of comfort for his friend. He hoped

that Pierre and the others would somehow forget with time. Seeing the terror in his friend's eyes and hearing the despair in his voice, he feared those men would never be the same again. Pierre would take the horror of Shabodun with him to his grave. Jacques wondered if he had done the right thing when he spared his life at the waterfall.

At the foot of the mountains, they constructed boats to carry them back to Avejion. The river was stronger than Jacques remembered. It flowed deeper and faster than it had in anyone's lifetime. Jacques realized the dragon had been at work a long time in these mountains. He weakened the people by withholding the necessities of life, then took control of their minds, bodies, and souls. His influence crept down the mountains and over the people slowly and without alarm. Like a cloud that grew wider and darker, it finally lifted.

They arrived home to a hero's welcome. Many of the people were unknown to the men, they were from the mountain and surrounding areas, now freed from Shabodun's influence. Jacques was shocked to find his wife, Viola, and his three daughters in a tent awaiting him. "I thought you were dead. I saw the dragon destroy the city. Nothing and no one could have survived in the city," he said, tears streaming down his face.

"Before the dragon attacked, I got a feeling. A voice in my head told me to take the people into the fields. It was your voice that woke me. We hid in the dried irrigation ditches. It was a terrible sight to see that dragon destroying our homes, but we all survived." Viola hugged him tightly to the point of choking the air from him, tears streaming down her face. For weeks she had held the fear that Jacques and the others had not survived. "When I saw the black smoke and heard the roar of the mountain, I knew you had defeated that horrid beast. But when you did not return, forgive me my love, I feared you were lost in the victory."

Jacques knew it was Aberash and Avia he had to thank for saving his family's life. They had left after the fighting started but not gone far. They were also responsible for bringing the others to Avejion. He thought, buried in the mountain, their powers were limited. But he was learning that distance or location had no effect on the maidens' abilities. They reached each other over a few miles or around the world, and the same held true for dragons, they all knew what had befallen their brother and by whose hand.

Jacques would need many people to build his castle, but that was not going to be a problem as more people were arriving every day. They couldn't explain why they were there; most had a strong feeling that Avejion offered safety and security. From what or why most did not know, others, those who had been touched by a dragon knew exactly why they were there. They were ready to take up arms for Avejion and the Dragon Slayer.

Napoleon the Dragon Slayer was admired and loved. He was crowned king as the first walls around the city went up. He would leave Shabodun in his ruby cradle buried in the mountain until the inner sanctum of the castle was secured. Then he and his brothers, for he trusted no others to the task, would retrieve the beast.

It took years to build the castle. It covered the original city and extended into the fields. The walls alone took a decade to erect. And the moat that surrounded the castle was filled with water from the mountain. The castle had three towers, one to the north, one facing the mountains to the east, and the last towards Rome. They were manned, always on guard for dragons. Within the castle's walls all manner of buildings were erected. Some of stone and mortar, others of wood and thatch. The main halls were made of stone three men high, quarried from the mountain and floated down the now powerful river. Made to stand against even the most powerful dragon and its terrible fire.

The city had expanded as well. It stretched westward towards the sea. Buildings and streets radiated out from the western gate. Every fourth road was a wide cobblestone thoroughfare that gave easy access to the castle. Avejion became a major city along the river that cut through the land. The river fed great fields of wheat and rye; orchards ran along both banks. And life slowly returned to the mountain as well. Trees sprang to life and in the foothill the people planted grapevines for wine making. Towns and cities dotted the riverside, life in abundance returned from its long absence.

. . .

One dark and moonless night, some twenty years after their battle in the mountains, the three brothers and an army of fifty returned to unearth the ruby cradle. As instructed by Apollonia, they carried with them a large iron box. Digging down to the tunnel took weeks and when they finally reached the dragon it was less than awe-inspiring. The chains and spikes lay around securing nothing. It didn't resemble anything that could suggest it had once been a fearsome creature. The dragon had been a hundred feet from nose to tail, claws that crushed a man in a single step, and a mouth that could swallow one whole producing a fire to incinerate everything in its path. The giant had been reduced to a lump of dull red rock an armful in size. It had no discernable shape, just rough edges and a sharp ridge that ran along its top. The brothers cautioned the men, "not a single drop of blood can be spilled upon this stone."

Although small as it was, it took a six-horse team and a system of pulleys to remove it from its crypt. Jacques noticed it was hot to the touch. Not hot enough to burn the skin, but enough to make someone unfamiliar with what was within fear its presence. Fear emanated from the stone. Paul felt the pull of the sleeping monster the most. It was eating away at his confidence every second he was in its presence. The dragon had turned to stone and was immobilized but it was far from powerless.

Ever careful of what was inside the rock, or more accurately what the rock was made of, they only attempted to remove it during the night. They placed it in the iron chest while still inside the mountain. Apollonia informed them that once reduced to the ruby cradle, a dragon would not have the strength to pierce the iron coffin. Not on its own. Then they sealed the iron box by immersing it in molten lead. The thick skin meant the box would never rust or be opened. Its smooth unadorned exterior gave no clue as to the power trapped within.

They returned to the castle under cover of night, and the lead encased iron chest that held the ruby cradle was buried under the dungeons. None knew which one and where, as the king had six identical lead covered boxes built and buried.

For six nights, he called twelve men, one at a time, to draw a sealed missive. Eleven told the reader to leave through the garden and throw the paper into the fire pit and never speak of this night. One missive was different.

Here is a key that opens two doors. One that leads to the foundation below.

There you will find a leaden chest. Find a spot and bury it waist deep. Make no notice where. The key will open another door to lead you out. Throw this missive and key into the fire and never speak of this night.

The one who read the message took the single candle and buried the mysterious box as instructed. On the seventh day, the foundation of the castle was filled with two feet of mud. Then precisely filled floor stones covered the entire dungeon level leaving no trace that anything lay below.

No man in his right mind would want to unearth such a thing, but men under the influence of a dragon were not in control of their minds. The King would gladly take the limited knowledge of the ruby cradle to his grave.

Twenty years he had seen peace. Avejion had grown into a wealthy kingdom. Her fields were prosperous. Many called it their home. Life was good under the flag of the Dragon Slayer, a winged serpent with a spike driven through its belly and out its back. The flag did not depict the battle as it was, but the spirit of what it took to defeat the dragon. Jacques and his men faced the beast head on and won. That is what the flag said to everyone who entered this kingdom.

Kingdoms to the west were happy to trade the bounty from the sea with King Jacques Napoleon. He was mindful of Apollonia's warning, though; he sent Peter to the north to begin a series of castles along the coast. He sent Paul to the east and had him start castles in the shadow of the mountains that separated East from West. They would need great fortresses of stone to defend against the dragons when they came.

News of great despair and great armies across the channel reached the throne of Avejion. There was talk of the Dragon Slayer in both the North and East. His kingdom was despised by those who sat on thrones in these other lands. Napoleon listened to his traders as to which kingdoms hated him, and which simply feared his name.

He knew those who hated him were under the influence of the dragon, Vargrerot. He wondered how long it would be before Vargrerot got up the nerve to move against him. He had learned a lot from Apollonia. He knew the dragons were eternal. But they were also impatient and acted on impulse rather than logic. His victory and subsequent prosperity antagonized the dragons. They were a jealous lot. And greedy. And vengeful.

They looked to destroy what they could not have. His kingdom which now covered most of Franco was larger than England, Prussia, Spain, and what was left of the old Roman Empire. He could feel the dark thoughts of invasion closing in around him. The skies were starless. Black clouds rolled across his lands. Fire rained down on fields and towns. His dreams of death and despair wracked him nightly. He wondered when the witch, Apollonia, would return or was this now his battle alone to fight.

She had warned him not to go looking for the dragons. It was better to wait for them to come to him. To fight the dragon and its people on his ground, it would be where he could draw them into a trap. They would wait until he was weak, maybe until he was dead, but they would come. Although, Apollonia most assuredly said, they would want to defeat him, not a descendant. The dragons were vain and vindictive. One would want to prove he was better than the others by killing Napoleon the Dragon Slayer. Even if it meant waiting until he was an old man before he attempted it.

Jacques knew something about the nature of his foe. He was not going to sit around and let his enemies decide his fate. He knew their weaknesses too and how to turn them to his advantage. Once his castles were ready, his brothers secured their defenses, Jacques sent minstrels into the lands to the north and across the mountains. They sang of the great battle and the tremendous wealth gained. He warned his minstrels to stay nowhere more than one night and tell no one where they were going next. They spread the tale of the Dragon Slayer across Europe and Asia.

Despite their precautions, most of the troubadours never returned home. In some cases, they were set upon by robbers or angry mobs. Others simply disappeared on the road. The men knew their job was to provoke the dragons. They were the first attackers in the war that was to come. And if they performed their task well the war would come sooner and on their King's terms.

Jacques raised a great army. He had forges turn out weapons of the finest steel through the process he learned from Apollonia. He also learned the composition of the black powder from Aberash. The black powder was not a weapon that could kill a dragon, but when used to propel an iron ball from a metal cannister mounted on the castle's walls, it would surely turn it back. The cannon was Paul's design and he placed them on top of the walls and at strategic points in the walls to protect the castles. Anyone trying to cross the bridge to the gates of the castle would face their brand of fire.

CHAPTER 10

THE AGE OF KINGDOMS

Jacques received news that other lords and kings throughout the British Isles had taken up arms against one kingdom in particular, that of Edward the Confessor. The king, with no heirs to the throne, seemed to be the perfect candidate for the intervention of Vargrerot. The defeat of Shabodun instilled fear in the older dragons. Men, with the aid of maidens, were a real threat to them. Edward's kingdom was in the flatlands. Vargrerot abandoned his mountain lair since men had the black powder from the kingdom of the East.

Although some of his brethren maintained a mountaintop hideaway—not as elaborate as Shabodun's—to put as much distance between them and their nemesis, the maidens. It didn't suit Vargrerot, as flight was no longer available to him. The long trek up the mountainside was arduous and riddled with ambush points. Instead, he took to building large castle complexes, a maze of buildings, towers, tunnels, and walls. Castles and fortresses dotted the English landscape. The people were pressed into laborious service for years. Cutting huge stone blocks from quarries with iron chisels, dragging them for miles with the aid of horses, finally refining, reshaping, and placing them in position. And when not enduring the back-breaking labor of building a castle, they were forced to defend it.

To attack the kingdom of Edward the Confessor was to engage in years of long struggles that provided Vargrerot with the sustenance he desired most, human flesh. Archers defended the walls from the towers with crossbows firing a dozen arrows at a time. The fields beyond the walls were littered with wounded soldiers. And the dark waters of the moats presented the greatest danger to attacking armies. The dragon would leap from beneath its placid surface and devour the troops in a moment of unimaginable fright.

Vargrerot the Wingless was known in the British Isles as the Sea Serpent of Wessex. Many believed he lived in the sea around the British Isle and was called to battle by the king. They also believed him to be a great spirit warrior sent to protect the king. Truth, he lived in the towers and grand halls above the throne rooms in the castles and made his way through the tunnels into the moat. Neither did he serve the king nor offer him protection. The king was his prisoner as were all his subjects.

Edward was commanded, and he obeyed, to wage war on the neighboring kingdoms in the guise of unifying the country. The wars were merely a means of keeping his dragon master fed. Vargrerot required great amounts of blood to satisfy his thirst, and it didn't matter whose blood he consumed as he frequently informed Edward. Without the ability to fly and absorb energy directly from the sun at high altitude, he needed a massive amount of food to maintain his strength. This land, the people, its kings and peasants, were his to do with as he pleased. Here, he reigned unchallenged by dragon or maiden. But not a sun rose or set that he did not keep his eyes to the south, across the channel.

Over the years, Jacques had made concessions to the Norsemen. Parts of Peter's land had been invaded and taken over by them. He felt the hand of Deyhezas at work. Jacques had acquired much knowledge from his brief time with Apollonia. He learned a great deal more about the nature of the dragons from the dragons themselves. It wasn't conscious knowledge he had gained, it was like a baby learning to walk, one day you simply know how to do it. Apollonia had opened his mind to their form of communication. He could feel their thoughts from time to time. He thought it was the benefit of keeping his prisoner beneath his feet. He learned to listen in on their arguments and petty squabbles. He knew the dragons would more than likely battle each other if given the chance. The lesser dragons were always ready to challenge one another for power. Their masters' intent was to let them battle and build up their strength before devouring them.

Instead of fighting to keep the dragons from taking more of his lands, Jacques launched an invasion force against the English. When Edward died on January 5th, 1066, his brother-in-law, Harold, took the throne. Vargrerot had built England into a formidable prize and favoring Harold Godwinson over his brother was the catalysis Jacques needed to spark a war.

Peter sent the Duke of Normandy, William, to lead his forces. The Norwegian King, Harald Hardrada joined forces with Tostig, Harold Godwinson's brother, the Anglo-Saxon King, to depose him. Harald III of Norway was more likely aligned with Deyhezas than acting out of his own ambitions, but the war removed him from Napoleon's lands.

The Vikings showed their allegiance to their dragon lord by carving their ships with his image. On their shields and armor, they displayed Deyhezas' head and face. He had promised the Norsemen the world, and they were willing to conquer it for him. Not since the Roman Empire had a people been so thoroughly seduced and corrupted by the power of a dragon.

Jacques had become adept to the politics of rule and war. He kept a wary eye on who his allies were and who his enemies could be. He let war weed out those who were the most dangerous to him. Deyhezas wanted war and Jacques was willing to give it to him. A war he could be proud of, against his old enemy. Jacques knew all about the centuries of feuding between Vargrerot and Deyhezas. He used it to turn Deyhezas' attention away from his victory over Shabodun. He had promised Tostig and Hardrada his support as they battled the English at Fulford. With Norman archers, a hundred arrows flew for each English knight fielded, they won a decisive victory.

Emboldened by their victory, and probably misled by Vargrerot, the pair advanced their armies to Stamford Bridge, a low-level waterfall which was easy to cross. They had planned to take York. The English had been alerted to the Viking forces and surprised the invaders on the riverbanks. Battle plans and secrets were hard to keep. Any dragon could reach into the mind of men, the more powerful the dragon the further away from the battle-field he could be and still see what was going to happen.

Vargrerot could taste his old adversary in the flesh of the

soldiers he feasted on. He had waited a long time to take his revenge. He wanted Deyhezas to come and face him, so he made his victories slow and painful. Tempting Deyhezas, as he seemed to be failing once again.

Vargrerot, you are too old and feeble to match wits with me and my men. Lay down your arms and I will absorb you. Add your life to my greater glory.

A Norse axman held the English at bay for hours. Every swing of the massive two-headed axe cut through armor, mail, and flesh. He was seven-two and broad-shouldered. He towered over the English as part man, part giant. Clearly, the spawn of some dark magic. He held the long thick wooden handle with both hands, slashing the weapon in a crisscrossing fashion. He severed arms, legs, and heads as the axe acted like a pendulum arching from high to low and back again. Every man who ventured onto the bridge, regardless of whether he carried sword, shield or lance, met the same end. The Norseman fell one hundred and forty men with his battle axe on the narrow stone crossway. His thick armor repelling arrows and deflecting spears. The morning passed into late day before they could surround him and drive lances into his back.

He gave his countrymen the time they needed to form their defenses. They managed to get ropes across the river and pull barges of wooden barricades into place. Ten-foot wooden spikes stuck out and up from the barges, shields bearing the Viking Clans hung between the spikes. Archers fired arrows through the gaps and then took shelter. Axmen and sword bearers charged forward as the English came into range and fell back behind the wall as another wave of fighters took their place. Hundreds, if not a thousand, a mass of men clashed on the river-bank. Hacking and slashing, stabbing and impaling, battling back and forth for seven feet of blood-drenched earth. The Vikings' shield wall held for hours against the English attacks. The English forces were badly outnumbered and dwindling. The battle would have been unwinnable if not for Vargrerot the Wingless.

Vargrerot was a pitiful broken figure of his former self. Without wings to soar into the sky where he could absorb the most power, his strength gave out quickly. England was a cold and cloudy land. Many times, the fields were shrouded in dense fog, little sunlight reached the dragon during these crucial times. He had taken to revealing himself to the enemy as even in this form he was terrifying to men. The massive armor of his black scales was now brittle and left him vulnerable. His body still gave protection from the arrows and spears, forming a moving wall twenty feet long. As he snaked his way closer to the enemy's position, his men uncovered firing arrows and slinging stones. He took the lead against the Vikings' shield wall using his fire to keep them hunkered down. Long trenches of sharpened poles protected the Norsemen in alternating and overlapping rows. They moved from one barricade to another, trying to escape the flames of the dragon. They were well trained in the battle tactics of the dragons by their master Deyhezas.

Then Vargrerot shattered sections of their fortified defenses with his spaded tail and razor-sharp six-inch claws. As they were pushed back, they left behind their armor to cross the river. Those who didn't have time or forethought to shed the heavy metal found themselves stuck in the mud and mire. Immobilized, they were easily picked off by the charging horsemen. Others were snatched up by Vargrerot. He chewed them noisily and spat their mangled bodies at the fleeing Norsemen, terrorizing them.

Deyhezas, is this the best force you can muster? I thought your Viking warriors were the most vicious fighters this world has seen. They scatter like sheep before my English wolves.

Finally, the English Calvary and infantry split the forces of Hardrada and Tostig. The sun was sinking behind the tree line, King Hardrada ordered his army to move into the forest and regroup. He hoped the shadows would give added coverage, and in tight quarters axe and sword would prove most effective. But the Englishmen knew the country and the lay of the land, they quickly took the high ground and resorted to the long bow. They laughed and casted wagers as to whose arrow would kill King Hardrada. They made target practice of him and his men. Arrows, silent and deadly, zipped between the trees piercing armor with ease. The archers firing only at the profiles of a man where he was least protected by steel breastplates.

Tostig Godwinson's fate was worse. His forces, reduced to half their numbers tried to form battle lines in the open fields. Against mounted lancers it was futile. The horsemen formed a line two hundred yards away, just the right distance to bring the horses to a full gallop. With reigns in one hand and shield and eight-foot lance in the other, their charge was unstoppable. The first wave impaled many and trampled those who stood to oppose them, then they returned with swords in hand to slash their way through the hapless foe. Orders were given to save Tostig for last and the cavalry men rode past him, withdrawing their blades. In minutes, his troops lay around him. He circled and lashed out wildly as the horses trampled over the fallen. Finally, one soldier came at him from behind and kicked him in his head. Godwinson struggled in the muck that once was his troops to regain his footing. But it was too late as each man dismounted and took a turn striking a blow. He was an Englishman who turned against his country, and for that he was hacked to death by his countrymen.

With the loss of thousands of men and hundreds of ships that were set ablaze in the English Channel, the threat from Deyhezas to the French was all but over. If he was to have a victory it would have to come at the expense of the English. He would have to commit to the conquest of England and give up his hold on Jacques' lands across the Channel. William the Conqueror took his forces to battle the weakened English troops at Hastings.

Vargrerot was weak and suffered many wounds in the battle against Deyhezas' forces. Consuming the Vikings and English soldiers provided much needed nourishment, but it did nothing to heal him. It would take months for him to recover. Time he did not have, the war was ongoing. For him to regain his full strength and health, he needed the Molytans' power but so many had been turned to dragons already. The rest have been taken by Apollonia. The Sea Witch still held them captive. He heard she had made a deal with Deyhezas, he would leave the Dragon Slayer's lands in peace, and she would return her hostages. William the Conqueror was to make the exchange and at the same time take what was Vargrerot's for Deyhezas.

He knew the maidens and men could not be trusted. Together

they formed a formidable force. They had captured Shabodun. He had grown enormous and dominant from the dragons he conquered and absorbed over the centuries. His power, perhaps, only rivaled by Deyhezas. Yet, he fell victim to the cunning trap of maidens and men. They could not be trusted but he was smarter, having defeated many armies with less power than any other dragon had made him so.

This was Vargrerot's chance to defeat Deyhezas or at least take what was due to him for so long. He would capture the stolen Molytans. Regain his health and strength. He would put an end to the Norsemen of France and Deyhezas, if he dared to show himself in battle. Deyhezas was ancient and bloated from centuries of idleness. He had long ago retreated from the battlefield, letting lesser dragons take his place. Now, his minions had plans of their own and he would have to collect the golden treasure himself. For none would turn over the Molytans once in their possession.

However, Hastings was not the same battlefield as Stonebridge. It was wide open, and the Normans had plenty of room to maneuver on horseback. Still, he held them at bay during the day-long battle. Although William outnumbered the English, they were battle-hardened and held their lines. The battle raged for hours as swords and shields stood firm for each side. Then night began to fall, and his strength faded with the sunlight. Vargrerot turned the night to his advantage as he was impossible to see in the dark. Vargrerot's footsteps made a squishy whisper of a sound on the blood-soaked field. He was upon their positions when the red of his eyes appeared. Only his fireballs marked his position. A few last blasts of fire sent the Normans fleeing in terror.

William's troops seemed to have had enough and began fleeing the battlefield. Perhaps, giddy with the sense of victory yet again, or blinded by the bloodlust of battle, King Harold's troops gave chase. The fog of war consumed them, and they pursued a small fraction of William's army. The major force regrouped and readied themselves for the final assault.

His armies left him and then Vargrerot realized the Sea Witch had made no such deal with Deyhezas. She was not on the battlefield or even in this land. She used the Normans' quest for land and power to draw him out. Now, he was surrounded by men and steel. They set upon him with pikes and iron netting. He fought through the night but without wings to take flight he could not outrun the cavalry and infantry. His attempted escapes were blocked and cut off by the Viking warriors. They circled and charged on horseback and by foot. Each man stabbing at him from behind. They avoided the only weapon he had, his dreaded flaming breath. And it grew weaker with each strike and wound he suffered.

What the dragons failed to comprehend, and the maidens used to their advantage, was that once the minds of men were conditioned to follow the thoughts of another, it was easy for the maidens to usurp their hold over them. Especially when the orders they were given were in line with their masters. Vargrerot, bleeding and wounded, was bound with chains and hitched to a team of a dozen horses. William's men, under the direction of Apollonia, dragged and walled him in a dark dungeon in Hampshire Castle, one of his strongest and most elaborate citadels, where without blood or sunlight he shrank into his ruby cradle. The tunnels that led to the secret room were collapsed and filled in with stone and earth. Apollonia then wiped clear the minds of his captors to ensure he would remain there for all time.

The Normans turned on their pursuers, who without clear battle lines and the protection of their dragon were now vulnerable to the greater numbers of their opponents. William's troops massacred Harold's forces and took his head on the battlefield. William the Conqueror was later crowned as King of England.

Deyhezas did not show himself on the battlefield those days and was deprived of adding Vargrerot's lifeforce to his own. Vargrerot's defeat meant he would threaten the world no more. Deyhezas, on the other hand, had gained control of the British Isles and the Northlands. He was sure to make his presence and power known throughout Europe. Jacques Napoleon had only removed him from his lands, not from his life. And since a dragon's life is eternal, the war with this one would be fought by his successors as well.

There were battles and raids by both sides across the channel. Thus, a hundred years of war began. Castles were under siege for months until either hunger, sickness, or weather forced the attackers to retreat. Each new year brought forth an advancement in weaponry, from siege towers designed to allow infantry to scale the walls, to catapults and trebuchets made to bring the walls crashing down. Jacques and his brothers' strongholds were impossible to defeat thanks to the black powder and guns hurtling iron balls at their enemies. They kept his lands free of dragons.

Armor also got better, going from simple mail covered by leather garment and metal plating to full suits of steel. Weapons of mace and lance became more effective but never replaced the sword. The sword had transformed as well, harder, lighter, sharper blades made of steel flashed on the battlefield like lightning bolts. The men could wield the weapons longer and fought with greater voracity than ever before. Armies swelled in size as professional soldiers and knights were supplemented by conscripted villagers. War became a business.

Napoleon the Dragon Slayer had defeated one dragon, and a second through proxy, but he had not stopped them from their goal. Their influence was felt farther than at any time in history. The Roman Empire had lasted a thousand years. The Chinese Dynasties for at least three thousand years. But now they were spreading everywhere, not one controlling force, but multiple and divided powers. From north to south and east to west castles and fortresses were going up. Great walls divided the lands and demarcated one dragon's territory from another. And between them pockets of men struggled to be free.

Napoleon sat in his throne room tired and exhausted from decades of battles. *Has all this been worth it? So much bloodshed and nothing has been gained.*

The Molytans you rescued have slowed the spread of the dragons. It appears they are great in numbers because so many men fall prey to their influence. Blinded by the promise of a golden crown and power has driven men to destruction. It would have been much worse if you had not defeated Shabodun. Apollonia reached out to him in his moments of despair. She had long ago left his land but never was he alone. She was a comfort and a curse.

He longed for her, but it could never be satisfied. *How much longer can this go on?*

They turn on themselves away from the battlefields. She assured him.

She felt the pain he carried each time he marched his men into battle. Every arrow that pierced a heart, each sword that severed a life from this world was a wound to her too. And yet she spurred him on, directing him as to which kingdom was the weakest, which was ready to fall. The costliest battles were when a dragon came to destroy the Dragon Slayer.

Men and maidens dressed in full armor faced the fire all day and into the night. Wearing the dragons down until they could be caged, chained, and carted away. The old dragons were too weak to escape, and the young, were too inexperienced to know when the tide of battle had turned against them. And each time a dragon was taken, it was locked away in a dungeon or windowless tower. Often, those of their own creation. And once they had been reduced to their dormant state, the men sealed the ruby cradles in iron and lead.

They search and accuse each other of hoarding the Molytans. It won't be long before they take to outright combat. However, that would not be to our advantage. It is better for us to defeat them one by one. Each time a dragon defeats another our chance of success diminishes.

So, you have yet to take the creatures to safety?

It is the only way to bring the dragons out of hiding. The lure of the Molytans' lifeforce is too great a temptation for a dragon to pass up. Elsewise, you would have to fight them in their stronghold, and your losses would be greater still. But now their numbers have dwindled and soon the Molytans will live in peace. Without fear of being transformed into the malignancy of the dragons. Then reason and sensibility can rule the world.

CHAPTER 11

RETURN TO THE SEA

One Eye Jack had a traveling troubadour camp, with six wagons. He made an invention, the iron horseshoes, for the cavalries of various kingdoms. The shoes were harder and more durable, allowing the horses to carry the greater weight of the armored knights a longer distance, making his horseshoes in demand across Europe. He used a new form of fire-making with a material discovered in China called coal. As a blacksmith, he was well known for the strength of his steel. His armor and swords were the best due to the heat of the coal fire which Jack amplified by blowing air under the coal with a foot pump.

The women used the same foot pedal device to operate their looms, making their cloths faster and the weaves tighter. Their garments were high quality. They made all types of clothes, fine silk dresses for the ladies at court, and heavy wool tunics for soldiers.

While in camp, his troop of men and maidens performed songs and poetry that told of the great battles and loves among the High Courts. They lifted the spirits of the people, relieving them of their darkest fears. Every place they visited had seen the destruction of war. The kingdoms of Europe and Asia were in a constant struggle for land and power. Kingdoms, some as small as a few thousand people and only a couple of hundred square miles sprang up overnight in the valleys and were just as quickly overthrown by their larger neighbors over the next rise. Or they absorbed another principality and grew to dominate an area. The landscape was in relentless flux and turmoil. The people were pulled in one direction then another. Their loyalties given to the strongest at that moment, the man who could raise the biggest army and wielded the strongest steel.

Jack also served as a healer, using techniques made popular by both the Chinese and Arabs. He mixed herbs and minerals to cure diseases and sicknesses. His potions were well known throughout. Apollonia and her maidens used the Molytans' power to enhance their curative powers. They used the power of the Molytans to quicken the recovery of those wounded in battle. But some wounds no potion or powder could remedy. He gained favor of kings, who readily provided information about their adversaries.

Sisters, we must be careful when offering aid to these soldiers. We cannot save everyone we meet, and there are eyes everywhere.

But we cannot let those we can save die. Objected Avia. She let her emotions and attachments sway her judgement.

The young soldier held her hand, and she channeled energy from the Molytans hidden in their cages in the only wagon made entirely of iron. The wagon had a single door with three massive bars and locks, and a small hatch on the roof which locked from the inside. Because of its colossal size it needed a six-horse team to pull it. Everyone believed it was Jack's money vault, they did not know its occupants were more precious than gold.

True, sister, but we should draw on the Molytans' energy once the sun has set, and their masters are dormant. To call upon them when the sun is high is a risk we cannot afford. You put the soldier's life in danger, our lives in jeopardy, and risk all that we are trying to do for the Molytans.

Sister, his oppressor is caged and in chains. He fought courageously to deliver us this victory. This man has earned our gratitude and care.

You have much to learn about treachery, my young one. One dragon's defeat is but his master's opening for attack. Do what you must for this soldier but do it quickly.

Aberash used her powers to counter the effects of her sister. The soldier was healing from his battle wounds, but he could not feel it. Thus, blocking his mind from the probing of the dragons. She understood the dragons used the suffering of men to locate them and hone in on their precious cargo. They inflicted bites on some during battle, which bonded the men's minds ever closer to them as they wallowed near death. The maidens were the only hope they had of surviving and their cure was a beacon to their tormentors.

They had been on the move since their battle with Shabodun. Six more maidens had joined them. Apollonia needed their energy to remain on land. The other maidens took turns returning to the sea and rejoining the group at the various castles. They kept their true nature hidden from men; Jack was the sole person who knew where they came from. His soldiers were oblivious to their disappearances, as there were always nine women with the troop.

Apollonia masqueraded as his wife and the other eight as his daughters. They formed their triads late at night to pass their life-force onto Apollonia under the full moon. A blue-green mist would rise from the ground and envelope the maidens. Apollonia and her daughters in the center circle while the other six would form a larger circle around them. Each maiden placed their two middle fingers on the temples of the ones next to her. Their other three fingers pointed upwards drawing in energy. An unbroken chain that channeled the power inwards to their matriarch. They performed the ritual each month and when they could, within a body of water as it amplified the effect of the lifeforce transference. They were careful to place the men in their caravans in a deep sleep before beginning the hallowed ceremony. None were aware of the true nature of Jack's business. He was called Jack of All Trades because there was no job they failed to do for their hosts. He was a confidant to kings and peasants and learnt as much in the halls of courts as in the taverns of towns. Always keen to the stories of strange happenings and unnatural occurrences.

He had been charged with keeping the Molytans safe by Jacques. Jack and Apollonia, in addition to guarding the Molytans, used them to tell when a dragon was nearby. The Molytans' life energy spiked when they came within a few miles of a dragon. Apollonia would then relay the information to Jacques. Together, they coordinated attacks on the dragons' strongholds. With their superior weapons and intelligence, they moved all around Europe, Asia, and the Northern Realms trapping dragons and forcing them into their ruby crystal state, thus freeing the remaining Molytans.

Apollonia stood on the shores near Gibraltar. A mist gathered on the sea and within the mist appeared a ship. The Molytans cannot touch water. To transport them to an island, specifically for them, she needed a ship. Her sisters would be her crew. They kept the ship hidden from the eyes of the dragons who searched her out every day.

She had not let her guard slip once since the Molytans had come into her possession. They remained in their cages, receiving sunlight only from the noon rays. Apollonia opened the roof hatch as the sunlight passed over it. It was long enough for the Molytans to maintain their health. She wished she could free them, but they would be drawn to the dragons as the dragons were to them. Their only hope was an island so far from any other land that no dragon or Molytan could make the flight. On an island, the Molytans would be incapable of leaving.

It had taken the maidens decades to find such a place. They found a chain of islands in the Pacific Ocean, volcanic in nature, tiny in size, three were dormant and barely noticeable to passing ships. There was no vegetation on them to attract anyone's attention. Barren and inhospitable, they would make the perfect hiding place for the Molytans.

Now, the reign of dragons could be brought to an end. The last few years had seen three more dragons trapped in their ruby cradles. Jacques' knights had faced down the fire and fury of the beasts with horses, lances, and shields. The din of battle, which made weaker souls afraid of facing their mortality, silenced only by the roar of the dragons. But for those who had faced the dragons before neither the cries of the dying nor the bellowing of the beasts turned them away from the victories at hand. With the power of the maidens to strengthen them, Jacques' knights triumphed in unwinnable situations. The cacophony of steel sword on shield and the swarm of armies in mortal contest were likened to a heavenly choir of dancing angles casting out the devils from paradise.

Apollonia took great pleasure in finally trapping Deyhezas in his castle. The siege lasted for a year and a half. Deyhezas could have escaped several times. As Jacques' armies battled the Norsemen and English, he fled from one castle to another. Each defeat freed more men, the great weight of his presence lifted from their minds, they joined their liberators in pursuit of their former master. Deyhezas fed not only off the dead and dying, but he drew power from those he held in captivity. Without the Molytans, he feasted on their adoration and servitude to him. And when it appeared that Deyhezas was ready to flee the battlefield, Apollonia or Aberash would join the fight, making themselves a target he could not resist. Finally fleeing when his castle was overrun, and the soldiers clamored for his death. He often fled under the cover of darkness when he was at his weakest, and none could see his black skin in the night sky.

They chased him to Kebnekaise Mountain in northern Sweden. His castle was built between the mountain's two peaks that stood six thousand feet above the sea. A distance Deyhezas felt was safe from the sea witches and their influences. But being so far north in the Arctic Circle meant the cold air helped to sustain Apollonia and her daughters without the sea. The air was heavy with life-giving water that the men found unbearable. The ice proved to be Deyhezas undoing, it sapped his strength even in the bright sunlight. The land was rich with forest and provided ample wood for catapults. They set a line of them on each peak. The castle had no doors or entrance accessible for a hundred feet from the ground. No siege tower could reach the openings high on the tower. This was a castle built for a dragon alone.

The men fashioned iron nettings that were launched over the top of the single tower castle as the siege began. These draped down over the three opening with links too thick for Deyhezas' fire to melt. For weeks the troops launched their nets shrouding the top of the tower in a black veil. Each net had been embedded with hundreds of iron hooks the length of a man's arm that the men called, "dragon claws." They gouged into the stone and caught the netting links to form an impenetrable barrier. There was no escape for Deyhezas.

Then began the bombardment of boulders. The catapults sent an unending barrage of stones. Day and night, the pounding rang from the mountaintop. Black powder freed huge slabs of rocks from the mountainside. Each one stood as tall as a man and weighted more than ten. Each strike shook the castle to its foundation. The final blow struck near the southern base collapsing the single tower castle in a white cloud and deafening roar.

The tower was made of such large stones and was hundreds of feet tall that the men found it impossible to retrieve Deyhezas' ruby cradle. When it collapsed, it covered the valley floor. They left him under the tons of rock and iron netting as this was as good a tomb as any they had planned. To be sure no one would ever try to reach him, Aberash used the last of the black powder to cause an avalanche of the mountain's snowcap that filled the valley. Over time a glacier would form burying Deyhezas for good.

Now, only the father of them all, Ehecatl remained. He was old and weak. The maidens would be able to trap him and once within the ruby cradle no one would be able to release the dragons again.

The ship silently nestled against the dock. The first rays of the day had not yet awakened the villagers. Apollonia led the wagon out of the barn. She felt a sudden stir in the air. The sweet smell that came after a spring rain filled her nostrils. She knew instantly a dragon had found her.

Ehecatl swooped down, ripping the main mast from the ship with a crackle of thunder. He took it aloft and dropped it vertically down in the center of the ship. The ship recoiled with an explosive boom. Water gushed up through the center. The ship barely remained intact as it sank. Maidens flopped on the dock and beach, unable to maintain their human form having been wounded by the attack.

Ehecatl made another drive, this time for the wagon. He sank his three-feet talons into the metal, then flapped his wings hard to lift its ponderous body a few feet off the ground. He twisted and ripped the wagon in half with his three talons on his hind legs as the horses pulled away in fright. The wagon cracked like an egg as it landed on its side. Apollonia had never seen Ehecatl. No mermaid had.

He was the largest dragon she had ever seen. His body was twice the size of the ship he sank. The scales on his body looked like black stones from a castle's wall. His head as large as a house and teeth the size of a man. And as he soared above, his black wings and body cast a shadow across the land. Legend named him the Black Death because he caused total destruction wherever he went. A single fire ball razed entire cities. Ehecatl was known and feared all around the world.

Ehecatl grabbed two iron cages and took off into the sky. A second later he returned for another pair. Black eyes stared down his long snout at Apollonia. Flames and smoke billowing from his nostrils into yellow orange clouds. Not from the stress or strain of the task he performed, but as a warning not to attempt to prevent his mission. He leaped effortlessly into the air with the heavy iron cages in his grip.

Fear not, Queen, I do not come for your life. I could take it at any time I wish but that would be too easy. You have more pain ahead of you.

Then he turned his head backwards and sprayed the remaining six cages with flames. Fire swirled around the cages inside the wrecked wagon and was sucked into the cages. Each cage contained two Molytans, they fought for the energy of the dragon's fire. The Molytans inside began their transformation. Frightful screams add to the chaos of those fleeing the port fearful of Ehecatl's return.

The cages could not hold the creatures as they grew. They doubled in size every second. The iron bars burst and rolled to the ground around them. Their skin thickened, and the glow of their life force was swallowed up inside their chest. A faint red mark on the young dragons' chests is all that is left of their former beings. They are hungry and in need energy.

Queen, you believe you can defeat me and my kind. I rule this world! Feed, my children. There are plenty of fishy women to satisfy you. Eat and grow strong.

The twelve dragons did as commanded by Ehecatl. They leapt on the maidens on the beach. One bite was enough to cut a maiden in half. The dragons fight over their victims like a pack of wild dogs, ripping and tearing the mermaids apart. Some launched themselves towards the sea only to be snatched out of mid-air and tossed into the waiting jaws of death. Their screams joined with the grunts snarled of the newly formed beast in the nightmarish scene.

Apollonia was powerless to save her maiden sisters on the beach. Those on the dock managed to roll into the lifesaving water before the dragons could discover them. She managed to narrowly escape the feeding frenzy back into the sea. She was joined by Aberash and Avia who were on the ship but leapt to safety moments before the mast hit. A dozen other maidens came to Apollonia's aid. She had been out of the water for such long periods of time over the years that her transformation to her natural form was slow and painful. Unable to swim they pulled her away from the shore where the dragons started to breathe fire as their transformation was complete. They burned the city to the ground before flying off in different directions after the frightened people.

Her recuperation would take decades if not centuries. She knew the world would be in terrible danger now that Ehecatl had the Molytans. And with a dozen new dragons fighting for power, the wars would escalate. A dark time was ahead for all.

Apollonia had underestimated Ehecatl. He let the others fight and battle for supremacy while he held the upper hand. Not seeking power or land for himself, he simply made sure the dragons' reign of terror would not end. With the new young dragons carving up Africa, Asia, and Europe the struggle would go on for centuries.

She left the world of men worse than it had ever been. The maidens continued to battle alongside the men when they found a leader they could trust. Many men fell to the temptations of their world and the promises of the dragons. And as a result, many maidens, labeled as witches, fell too. The dragons made it a point to burn them at the stake whenever possible. Dragons learned to work in secret, to cast their influence from the shadows. And most importantly, not to engage in battles amongst themselves. It took three hundred years of constant war before one man rose again in the land of Napoli. A baron from the line of Napoleon the Dragon Slayer came to power. He had an honest heart and more importantly a strong mind.

Apollonia had spawned three more daughters by this time, Rehema, Raakel, and Raanan. Aberash spawned daughters of her own and they were deeply committed to the war. While she avoided getting drawn into wars of men. She tracked the dragons from Africa to Asia, making bonds with men as needed, directly battling the dragons near water. The maidens found the dragons could not survive under water and with enough of them they could overpower the dragons beneath the waves. There, they quickly transformed to their crystalline state as their air and fire ran out.

Since dragons had made it their mission to destroy all the mermaids, Apollonia moved their home from the Mediterranean westwards to islands far from the reach of dragons. There the maidens lived in peace. The coral waters were warm and peaceful most of the time providing optimum breeding grounds for the mermaids. Few men had ventured this far west, and their kind offered no threat to the maidens of the sea. There was harmony among the people of the West, the corrupting power of the dragon had no effect on their lives. They feared not the invasion of dragons.

However, Apollonia felt it her duty to aid the men once more in their fight for freedom. She returned to the country of France as a young girl. The dragons would not recognize the eight-hundred-year-old maiden in this form. Her young daughters were unknown to them. They had learned to disguise their true nature from men and dragons. She rode under the banner of the Christians and was called Jeanne d' Arc.

She carried a sword and a spear whose head was formed from the star crystal. It was hard, sharp, and glowed with the power of virtue. It was the strongest element the earth could yield and had the strength to pierce the hide of the dragons. Under her leadership, Charles fought the English. She rallied the defeated forces of Charles' armies to impossible victories. Forcing the Englishmen from the land and capturing some of the warring dragons of Europe.

Each one captured was entombed and turned into their ruby cradles. The cradles were taken by men and hidden then their minds wiped clean of the memories. The dragons had tried and succeeded to free some of their captured kin, forming alliances, betraying and killing each other, and spreading chaos. The whereabout of the fallen dragons was therefore hidden from all but a few maidens. And no one knew the locations directly. Instead, a spirit globe of pearl—layers of the nacre excreted from mermaids—encased in calcium carbonate kept the memories of men and maidens. The pearl had a unique blue-green color from the different mermaids' aragonite as they added the information that stored the locations of the crystal ruby cradles they hid. The location of the pearl and how to retrieve the information from it was split between a few maidens so no one could be forced to reveal the information entirely.

CHAPTER 12
THE LAST WAR

Rehema shed a tear at the end of the tale.

Zabella felt weak and drained by the experience. "How is this supposed to help me?"

"You will find what you need in the memories." Rehema told her. "Look beyond their actions, search their hearts. Ehecatl has turned all the Molytans into dragons. And they fought for decades for supremacy. Some could not let go of their vendettas and as they defeated one another they absorbed their rivals. Always becoming more powerful. However, there are still more than a dozen left. Defeat them now and you defeat them forever."

Zabella exited Rehema's cave thirteen years older, and it showed. The re-living of lives brought the joys and the sorrows. What was theirs, became hers. She would reflect upon the events and find solace or madness in the world. Then it struck her, she needed a champion. Apollonia had found that champion in Jacques. She had to find one who was incorruptible, one who would be untainted by greed or the lust for power. A simple man with a simple goal, to save his world.

"Return tomorrow and your education will continue," Rehema told the young maiden.

"I thought you showed me all there was to know about the dragons?"

"You have seen all that ancient history has to teach you," Rehema informed her, "there is a modern history. Information that I know and learned from my sister, Aberash. Things I have learned from my battles with them. Information that will teach you how to kill the dragons."

"I don't think I am here to learn how to kill," Zabella said defiantly, "is that not what got you exiled here?"

"Yes, it is." Rehema locked eyes with the girl. "Look deep within yourself and you will see your father believes as I do. Dragons cannot be contained. They will never stop causing death and destruction in the world. It is what they are made for, why they exist. If one remains alive, in any form, then it will find its way back into this world and unleash hell upon it."

Zabella returned to her companions. Abagail waited all those years for her return. In that time, she had joined with many women far and near. Aberash had taught her how to search for important people, and be kept informed of what happened in the world at-large. How to use her powers to influence and guide them. Mermaids bonded to people's hearts. It was the strongest connection; dragons could only reach people's minds. She had bad news for her, "The Americans have turned to war. They fought through the most destructive four years of any nation on earth. The young nation is turning its attention to others in the west. Millions stand to lose their lives if they turn from freedom for all to imperial power."

There was little evidence of a dragon in the Americas. However, Zabella had learned enough to know their influence could be carried by others. Their influence was perhaps world-wide now. She was sure the New World would be dragged into the same morass of pain and suffering as the Old World. For thousands of years, death and destruction would flow as easily as the blood of men. The American Civil War had shown her that the weapons of war were spreading as quickly as the hatred in men's heart. Rifles had replaced swords on the battlefield as much as mercy was exchanged for mayhem. There was a blind-ness to the pain of inhumanity. Men had turned very dark within their souls. It had to be more than the influence of dragons. She had to return to Rehema and learn what darkness she had acquired over the centuries. And if she had unleashed that dark-ness on mankind. She knew Rehema still held great power. She might be physically confined to the island, locked in her human form, but she was not trapped there.

Zabella entered Rehema's cave at dawn.

The ex-Queen was waiting and ready for her. "You understand that the dragons can't simply be locked away. They have grown powerful inside their ruby cradles. Their influence in the world of man far outreaches their physical presence in this world. There will always be those whose weakness they will exploit. Through their cunning and guile, they push their slaves into positions of power. Others will always follow."

Rehema merely tapped the girl's temple and Zabella dropped to the ground, transformed into her maiden's body. She was instantly catapulted back in time. This time into Rehema's consciousness. She was a maiden about the same age as Zabella was now. She followed her mother to the shores of France. Zabella changed this time into a boy. She took the form of a young squire. She once again would see, feel, hear, smell, taste, experience every thought and emotion as Rehema did. She would live her life, starting with that terrible day in Rouen, France.

The morning was overcast by a haze of smoke. The all-too-familiar smell of gunpowder choked the lungs and grayed the sky. Cannons rang in the distance, far enough away not to be an immediate threat to life. A low whistling washed over the land as balls of red-hot iron large and small streaked near and far. The cannons had left their perch atop castle walls and had now made their way across the battlefields of the world.

They marched from China in the East to the French coastline. Once introduced to this land by the maidens they took on a power of their own. Growing and spreading like a malignant plaque, they infected and corrupted the armies of men. The maidens used them to inflict devastating blows on their foes, dragons, and topple their walls. Unfortunately, their killing power amplified the hold the dragons had on the kings of war. It allowed their armies to march without the protection of their masters, and still bring with them their terrifying might. Cannons and guns, fueled by gunpowder, were a hundred times more powerful than any dragon could be to the kings. They allowed the kings to raise large armies, because soldiers did not need as much training as archers or knights, and oppositely because more soldiers would be killed in battle. Hundreds turned to thousands. How could the maidens know the true consequences of bringing the black powder into the world?

Apollonia, in the personage of Jeanne d' Arc, had just about finished the task she started six hundred years earlier. Nearly all the dragons had been defeated. Encalais, was knocked out of the sky by a volley of a dozen cannon balls of iron and smooth granite as he tried to attack the castle Chinon. Castles were now built with round towers with sliding metal shutters to protect the men from the dragons' fire. One cannon mounted on a rotating platform could quickly attack the dragons from all directions. Some had two small cannons to fire in rapid succession, hitting the dragon as it attacked and tried to flee. Encalais suffered many broken bones and was rendered unconscious during the attack. Charles VII caged the wounded dragon and gave Jeanne la Pucelle, the name she preferred, consul of his freed army. She warned Charles to bury the dragon under his castle, but he refused.

"He'll serve a greater purpose on display. Show the people these beasts and their English lords have no power over the French Crown. He cannot escape. His fire is weak, and the chains hold his head to the ground. With Encalais in a cage, and you at the head of my army, the English and Duchy of Burgundy will be crushed."

"I have no doubt Orleans will be liberated. I will drive King Henry's forces back into the sea. But I beg of you, beware of the power of his dragon, his body is broken but his voice is still strong. Some will heed his call just as I obey the word of God!"

Apollonia inspired the army and the people in Orleans to rise up against the Anglo-Burgundian forces that had laid siege to the city. Few in numbers, they charged the troops. The guns of the English, of everyone, were less than accurate. Unlike the sword, it more often missed its mark. The French coulevriniers were most effective as a first use against a line of infantry. Then battles were decided by hand-to-hand combat. After shots were fired, the men returned to swords and daggers. Others used their various battle axes and spears. They fought with a new-found vigor and drove the enemy from the city. Fort after fort and city after city was liberated as she rallied the people along the Loire River. The French soldiers' war cry was louder than their cannons as the Maid of Orleans led them to decisive victories. And thanks to her, a new and honest king was crowned.

She thought victory was at hand, but she was wrong. She was betrayed. Encalais was worming his way into the mind and heart of Charles. "You have taken back your country. Crowned in Reims, even as your enemies surrounded you, powerless to halt it. The girl is of no use to you anymore. It is time for you to take command. You know there can only be one ruler, and as long as your men cheer her name, you will be King in name only."

"It is true, the people love her. But how can I betray that and still hold onto my people?"

"With peace, my King," Encalais counselled. "The people will do anything to have peace once again. They will accept anything that will put an end to the war. And if her virtue was diminished, they will praise you for having delivered them from her."

In a bargain for a lasting peace, King Charles VII of France turned her over to the English. He arranged for her capture by Burgundians' forces at Compiegne by withdrawing his troops from the battle. As the English advanced on her position, the flanking troops fled the battlefield. Rehema watched from a nearby hill as her mother foolishly remained behind with a small rear-guard troop of one hundred men. They surrounded and ambushed them. She was captured and handed over to Duke Philip of Burgundy for trial.

Apollonia attempted to escape her tower prison. She summoned all her power and did the one thing no mermaid would dare to do, she transformed into a condor and leaped from the window. Her arms thickened and shortened, her legs and torso too. The hair on her body transformed into feathers. She flapped and spread her wings to glide away from her prison. But she was unfamiliar with this creature. Being away from the sea for over a year left her weak and unable to maintain her shape. She plunged to the ground as Rehema, Raakel, and Raanan looked on helplessly. They could do nothing to save her as the soldiers dragged her back inside the castle to face her fate.

"I know who and what you are," began Duke Philip, "I can spare your life."

"I know what your master seeks. I will take it to my grave." *Do you hear me, Ehecatl! Neither I nor any of my sisters will ever reveal where your brothers are held.*

I am eternal. We are forever. In time we will make this world our own. You and your kin will pass from this world through flame.

Duke Philip said, "I will place you in a dungeon very close to the sea. The ocean spray will refresh you. Would that not please you?"

Where do you find such fools? You are all but alone in this world now. Your brothers will devour each other, and they will one day come for you. And whether it be you or one of your brothers who is the last of your kind in this world, my sisters shall take great pleasure in locking you away for eternity.

"I will make this promise to you now," the Duke spoke before the court, "instead of burning at the stake, you and all your sister witches can live out your lives in the dungeons. TELL ME, WHERE ARE MY MASTER'S RUBY CRADLES!"

The priests and noblemen of the court were alarmed by the Duke's outburst but said nothing. The Duke made more claims and charges of Jeanne d' Arc being an agent of the Devil. The voices she claimed came from God, her knowledge of her enemy's strengths and plans, her power over the French people and their king, all were proof of her Satanic union. "Reveal who aids you! Tell this court where your evil brood hides. Where can we find these sources of your demonic powers?"

Fool, she cannot tell, for she does not know. To the fire with her!

After learning that she did not know the resting place of his dragon kin, Ehecatl ordered Apollonia burned at the stake by his English brother. The wood pile was twice as high as it was for others who suffered this fate. And unlike the others, whose bodies were drenched in oil when tied to the stake, Apollonia was left dry. It meant she would cook before the flames consumed her. For Jeanne d' Arc, the Maiden of Orleans, savoir of France, the handmaid of God, death was slow and painful. And a delight to Ehecatl who had waited centuries to see her come to this end. He could only have been happier if it was his flame that ended her life. He did consider it.

Rehema, it is now your battle! Their evil is their weakness. Apollonia called out to her daughter through the flames to remain vigilant against the dragons and the evil they represented. *Their way can only survive if you allow it to. You and your sisters must stand together.* Then she yelled as the flames consumed her, "Jesus! Jesus! Jesus!"

To Rehema that meant fighting not just the dragons, but the men who would come under their control. She no longer looked to mankind for partnership. They were either her enemies in league with the dragons, or pawns to be used as she led her maiden army.

The men were easy to control by both sides appealing to the lowest instincts in them. Rehema found the maidens had a distinct advantage, though. Whereas, the dragons' greatest weapon was greed, maidens used their bodies and voices to stir the lustful hearts of men. And even though many of the maidens disagreed with her tactics, it worked. She raised enormous armies and launched great crusades, driving the dragons back into their dormancy.

It was Aberash who was given the greatest weapon against them. One of the last Molytans had given her an arrowhead made from the starstone, or as men called them, diamonds. The Molytan called the stone, "the dragon killer." He had learnt of the stone's power from Apollonia. Taken from deep within the earth, it was harder than any dragon's hide and could be made sharp enough to penetrate their heart. It had to be cut in just the right fashion, eight sides that came to a point.

Rehema used diamonds against Encalais. He would be the first to pay for her mother's death. But she vowed he would not be the last. She had just a small handful of them. She wrapped the stones in a small sack, packed them into the mouth of a culverin, and fired as he approached her in the halls of King Charles' castle.

He had remained small in stature to fool the king. Standing as tall as a small pony he was a perfect target. They ripped through him and the one that pierced his heart caused the dragon to burn internally. He was consumed in screeching agony by his own white flames, reduced to a pile of ash, and whisked away on the gentlest of winds.

Black powder, cannons large and small, had the power to change the world. Rehema knew how to use it. She immediately commanded her maidens to use men to unearth more of the starstones. Mining was a task only men could endure. The men eagerly obeyed as the diamonds' brilliance made it most valuable in trade. When confronted with these weapons, the dragons protected themselves by cocooning in their chrysalis. They learned to expel all their energy quickly and shrink to their rock-like form. The diamond shot inflicted pain, but by the dragons lacking energy, it was not lethal. They waited for the day when they would be free to terrorize again.

Once the war with the dragons ended, Rehema turned her ire towards men. She never forgave them for the betrayal of her mother. She made it her mission to seek out men who desired power and caused their downfall. After she became Queen of the Mermaids, she gathered a small group of her sisters in secret to perpetuate the myth of witches and their craft, the crime her mother had been charged with. She trapped many men and women in her schemes and led them to their death. Once the Old World was firmly set on a path of destruction, she left for the New.

Then, she fell in love with a man, David Cutter, a shipbuilder in the New World. David put aside the beliefs and ways of the Old World. This was a new land, new people, and new gods. Like so many who left, he sought his wealth in the riches of the land, not built on position or inheritance.

Rehema found the people of the western shores honorable. They respected the world and all those in it. They opened their world to the newcomers. Rehema presented herself as a great spirit of the sea in human form. For these New Worlders many spirits took physical forms when necessary. They were the bridge between the worlds.

David's clear-eyed outlook on equality and prosperity led him to start a shipbuilding business. His broad shoulders and strong back turned trees into lumber, wood into ships, fleets into commerce. He turned commerce into wealth for all around him.

One night, Rehema met the young visionary and was immediately taken in. After centuries of callous contempt, she found the one man who could be truly trusted. She helped him build his empire as his wife, keeping her true nature a secret.

But secrets have ways of finding the light. And once exposed, all involved feel the deepest wound to the heart. David was no different. The old-world prejudices slipped in and squeezed out the love and joy he knew with her. He turned her over to the religious authorities for witchcraft.

It was his betrayal of her, and his burning at the stake of two of her maidens that sealed her heart in darkness. She used her powers to continuously pit man against man and nation against nation. Much as the dragons had done, she drove wars that cost the lives of millions. Ironically, it was Aberash, the one who had found a way to rid the world of dragons, who brought them back, trading their freedom to stop her sister. What Aberash did not know was that the dragons did not sleep all those years. They had planned for the day they would return. They did not know where they were, but they were in constant contact. And so was Rehema.

She had one ruby cradle in her possession. She used it to spy on the dragons' thoughts, to learn their secrets, to be ready for their return. She learned how to manipulate men, to reach so deep within their psyche that her thoughts became theirs. She sowed seeds of hatred in men's hearts that allowed them to do cruelties normalcy would reject. And she learned where the dragons' power came from, how the lifeforce of the Molytan was transformed. She alone knew the secret of the dragon's fire.

Now, Zabella knew her secret. She heard the darkest thoughts of the dragons. The dark thoughts of the ex-Queen. She knew Rehema would use the dragons' power against the world of men. Use the dragons' power against them. If not for her father and her exile to this cave, she would have used her knowledge to devastate the world.

Zabella felt the ex-Queen was now using her to free herself from this prison. She was draining her power. Transforming herself. She was fighting to break the link before Rehema took everything she had and made it her own. Rehema would become her and she Rehema. She had gotten what she came for, but the price Rehema charged for that knowledge would be her life. Rehema was regaining her powers. Much like the dragons absorbed the life of their opponents, Rehema had been stealing her lifeforce.

Just before her mind was lost forever within the tangle of horrors that was Rehema, she thought of her father. Not a thought of him as she knew him, loving, happy, smiling. She had a thought she did not know she carried. A thought she did not know from whence it came. It was his thought. It was cold. It was black. Darker than any night she had ever known. More isolated than the deepest ocean she had swam. And now it was Rehema's.

The mind link ran both ways. She had felt and lived all that Rehema had done. And Rehema in return took her life on. And when she took on the death of the girl's father, a death Zabella did not know she carried within her, death Shera carried while she held her within her womb, death planted so deep within her consciousness that only Rehema could reach it. Although, her curse was that Jeremy couldn't die, he still felt death. Was cut off from any sensation of life, his heart did not beat, his lungs did not crave air. In time, his mind fell silent too, no thoughts filled his head. What he felt Shera felt, Zabella felt, and so Rehema died too. Whereas Jeremy had Shera to pull him from the darkness and restore his consciousness, Rehema had no one to bring her out of the grave. She trapped herself in unending darkness, devoid of thoughts or feelings, complete nothingness.

Zabella left the cave. Sixty years had passed since she arrived on the island. She spoke to the maidens who tended to Rehema, "your queen is gone. Your duty to her is complete. Rejoin your sisters now, there is much work to be done."

"You are not my queen," answered one of the mermaids. She spoke for all of them. "You are nothing more than an assassin sent to finish the work your mother started. We will stay and wait for Rehema to come back to us. If she does not, then we will form our own order. And you, none of you, can call us sisters."

"As you wish," Zabella conceded, "the storm will remain, in case you are right about Rehema."

The world tethered on the edge of conflict and war. Each one was more horrific than the last. Each spawned a new set of combatants. These were fought for land, money, power, gods. Some conflicts pulled in many different powers, building coalitions, lasting years. Others lasted months, with one or two colonial powers locked in battle. One war lasted mere minutes, when the British bombarded one Sultan's palace and replaced him with their choice for ruler. In the Americas, the United States went on campaigns of death against the indigenous tribes as they spread across the land. Many claimed victories. In reality, they were just a long succession of losses. No Winners. Zabella felt the influence of dragons in all these conflicts. Their force secretively corrupting and pushing men's thoughts and actions.

CHAPTER 13

QUEST ANEW

Zabella re-entered the world already embroiled in war. It was much different from the one she left decades ago. She left behind a world of colonial powers. Each trying to grab as much of the world and its people as a king could dominate. They were pitted against each other for their own selfish goals.

The world she returned to had become a mixture of alliances and unsteady partnerships. Kings and czars, chancellors and dukes found themselves bound by the mutual distrust of their neighbors and a century of conflicts over borders. Colonialism had been replaced by nationalism. A sense that their nation was the dominating force of the world and therefore its rightful ruler. She knew this was a misguided pride.

And Europe had seen another revolution. Although, it could be said its birth was in the Americas, the United States to be precise, it quickly spread. Industrialization had taken hold, and its greatest influence was felt during the War between the States. Cannons and guns had been on the battlefields for more than two hundred years, but up until then they were small, stationary, and slow to action. They were now massive, mobile, and especially in the case of the gun, mechanized. The machinegun, with its ability to fire in rapid succession, turned the gun into an efficient, easily operated, killing machine. This weapon was by far the greatest threat. It was the one reason peace was unattainable. The machinegun made it possible for a few to keep the war going no matter how atrocious the losses.

Zabella searched the hearts of men. From king to commoner there was one sentiment that was felt by all, glory was owed to him. The ranks of the armies had swelled two or three times what they had once been. People took to the notion of war as a rite of passage. A chance to prove their worth among men. Courage under fire had somehow replaced common sense.

"This is such a beautiful city and country. No wonder you wanted Bosnia to be part of the Austrian Empire," remarked Sophie Ferdinand as their carriage wound through the streets of Sarajevo.

"The Serbs and the Bosnian people have always belonged with the Austrians and Hungarians. We will build a mighty empire," replied the Archduke. "We will make the Russian Czar think twice about crossing our borders."

The rhythmic click-clop of the pair of horses, the roar of cheering crowds along the parade route, the festive sounds exalting the royal couple was shattered by two gunshots. A lone gunman leaped onto the running board of the carriage and fired point blank at Ferdinand and his wife, Sophie.

The assassination of Archduke Franz Ferdinand of Austria lit the fuse that ignited the powder keg that was Europe. Years of deals and alliances were put to the test. Leaders of Austria-Hungary and Germany, the Central Powers, launched offensives against Serbia, Belgium, and Luxembourg. Then Germany turned its attention towards its long-standing enemy, France.

The United Kingdom of Great Britain and Ireland joined forces with France and Russia forming the Allies Forces. Once enemies, France and Russia had a standing alliance to protect themselves from Germany who was standing up troops on each of their borders. England knew that if France fell, Germany would be just across the channel from the isle nation. It was the King's intention to stop Germany before it came that close. He thought that if war had to be fought it was better to fight it on the continent.

The Ottoman Empire joined the Central Powers, spreading the war into the Caucasus, Mesopotamia, and the Sinai. Italy left Germany and Austria-Hungary's Central Powers and joined the Allies to fight against Bulgaria. The war, it was thought, would be a quick affair as most wars were at the time. At its inception each side thought its superior firepower would allow them to overrun their enemy. However, this was not to be, the old strategies didn't consider the effectiveness of the new weaponry. Machineguns on the battlefields made all attacks a useless and futile effort.

Orders of, "OVER THE TOP, MEN!" sent hundred out of the trenches and into an unrelenting torrent of bullets. A tangle of barbed wire made a deadly maze that the troops had to navigate while dodging enemy fire. Most never reached their objective. And if they did, hand grenades, gas canisters, and flame throwers made the enemy's trenches theirs. Battle gains and losses were measured in a few hundred yards and thousands of dead. Victories were so costly, losses so heavy, neither side could sustain an advance. Stalemates across all fronts turned the war into a siege battle of old. More nations and states rallied to the Allies, either out of loyalty or necessities in Europe, Africa, the Middle East, and in the Pacific. Instead of castles being built, trenches were dug a few hundred yards from their enemy. Artillery shells rained down on the opponent's positions and the killing fields known to all as "no man's land" dominated the landscape.

Generals were sending their troops, millions in all, to battle, but Zabella felt the now familiar persuasion of the dragons. Having been released from captivity, they quickly started acting for their own self-interest, locked in a deadly struggle to claim as much as they could. Once, they waged wars to be the only survivor, destroy man and maiden, but now, all were driven to utter madness by the overwhelming flood of blood. They were determined never to return to their ruby cradles again. And that meant never engaging in direct combat.

All the dragons respawned as new beings. Vargrerot had returned to the world fully reformed. Both wings were strong, and he took to the skies with renewed purpose. Although he still craved Shabodun's blood, centuries of captivity tempered his vengeance. He and all his brothers knew there was a greater threat to their existence. The maidens were the only ones who could challenge their power by gaining control of men. Perhaps, the dragons realized that men and their weapons had become too powerful. Zabella sensed, for the first time, the dragons feared death.

Through his defeat and suffering, Vargrerot had become the strongest of the dragons. He commanded his brothers to locate and track the sea witches while he made his way across the Northern Tract. He needed an enormous amount of energy to make the trip to the New World. The sun's rays energized his body and mind.

He avoided the world of men and maiden, travelling the high mountain ranges northward, crossing mountain top after mountain top, living off the strongest rays of the sun. He forestalled his hunger and thirst to hide his true agenda. The New World had given rise to a new spirit of adventurers. They had yet to be exploited. No one had directly touched their hearts and minds. Their corruption would be easy. Here he would begin his empire. The others, dragons, maidens, and the old world of man, would be blind to his conquest.

Vargrerot would not spend his time in idle exile as Ehecatl had done. He intended to make his presence felt throughout the world. First, by eradicating the last of the maidens. They would be drawn to the aid of men and perish trying to save them. Then he would turn his power against his brothers. He would build alliances and single out those he would destroy, starting with Shabodun.

He flapped his wings once and raced hundreds of miles over the featureless snowfields. He exhaled a great plume of fire turning the white to blue beneath him. It quickly returned to the flat frozen plain before he was out of sight. He inhaled and again blew fire across the land and sea, growing in size and strength.

Each time he breathed in the frigid air and expelled the inferno that raged inside him, he stoked his own furnace with malice for the world. Although fully reformed and healed, he still felt the pain of losing his wings with each stroke through the sky. It was a mental pain he chose to hold onto, a reinforcement of his destiny to be the sole ruler of this world. He had battled many dragons and absorbed their spirits within him. He ripped their chest open and devoured their hearts. Their minds had long fallen silent and succumbed to his will. Their strength was his own. He came back into this world a massive version of his former self.

Mankind had proven to be a great, if unwitting, accomplice by building war machines the dragons never dreamed of. Black powder became gunpowder, and the gun went from the single shot of muskets to the Gatling gun to the machinegun. The Second Industrial Revolution was a boon to the manufacturing of steel and railroads. Powered by steam, gasoline, and diesel, the dragons created armies of factory workers to turn out ships, trains, and tanks.

Iron had once been their enemy, the dragons now showed men how to refine it into hardened steel more efficiently. With the maidens decimated by Rehema's wars, the dragons held unchallenged control over mankind. They used that control to feed their insatiable need for blood. They gave up sole possession of the skies and enjoyed men flying dirigibles and biplanes to spread death in the form of gas attacks and strafing runs.

This is an outrage. Captivity has made you all weak. Do you fear mankind so much that you sit idle while they invade our domain?

Deyhezas, what concern to us is a few men in these flimsy contraptions? They still do our bidding. They feed us daily. And at any time, any one of us can swat them from the skies with ease.

You are a fool, Shabodun! You have always been short-sighted. More concerned with your stomach than your future. Men are a clever beast, today they fly against each other. But there will come a day when they chase us across the skies.

And when that day comes, they will face my true fearsomeness.

Let's hope it is not you who is made to fear.

Zabella felt a very familiar darkness clouding men's minds. The power she had gained from her grandmother left no doubt that Rehema had a hand in the current situation. She had poisoned the minds of men before her exile as much as the dragons in their freed state. Rehema had used the powers of the dragons to burrow deep into the psyche, manipulate people from afar, even while she was in exile. And once she connected with her granddaughter, Rehema's attack on the world of men intensified. Zabella had been unaware of it at the time but now she felt the undeniable effects.

Zabella and her maidens searched for the dragons in the trenches taking on the forms of young soldiers. They expected to find them there feasting on the wounded and dying. But they were not in the trenches and dugouts of the frontlines. At night, the maidens made their way to the medical units behind the lines but again came up empty. Each maiden carried a pistol loaded with diamond-tipped bullets. After two years, long past the battles of the Verdun and Somme, which recorded millions of deaths, they realized the dragons would not expose themselves to battle. They had no need to; man had become so adept at killing they needed no help from them.

Once the war had started, and each side determined to win at any cost, the dragons had little more to do. Death had spread from the battlefields to the cities and towns. The bombardment of artillery laid waste for miles around. While the battles yielded no discernable outcomes, no victories, no defeats, they provided a bounty for the dragons. They waited for the armies to eventually move on and feasted on the carnage left behind. They could feed at will, wherever and whenever they wanted.

So many had fallen in battle, and no one came to claim them. Gone were the nurses in white with red crosses or crescents to pull the injured away to safety. If a friend did not retrieve a mate, then that person would die crucified on the wire. Occasionally, horse-drawn wagons would scour the deserted battlefields for weapons and the wounded. But the warhorses had a more vital task, pulling the heavy artillery. A job that claimed the horse's life in a month or two from sheer exhaustion.

This was not a war that was being fought for victory. It was fought to make the other side the greater loser. All the leaders knew at some point they would run out of blood to shed. The attrition of men and beast could not last forever. How long could it last was the unknown.

Zabella knew the Americans had pushed their boarders from ocean to ocean at the expense of the lesser developed natives' populations. The colonial powers had brought conquest and slavery to the New World. Now the New World, which had grown up in a hurry, was ready to take its place in this macabre theater. She felt there was little she could do to stop the madness.

She returned to Usea Maya where her mother, Shera, looking twice as old as she should have, was prepared to turn the throne over to her. Her father, Jeremy, was barely alive. He held onto life just long enough to see his daughter once more. She touched his mind one last time and found the pain of the world too much for him to bear. He was linked to all that was going on through her and her mother. He found no joy in living. Zabella and Shera laid him to rest in the garden behind the house where they had spent the last five decades.

A dark cloud hung over the island of the mermaids. With war raging all around them most of her sisters feared the dragon would soon send their navies to wipe them out. Zabella wondered if this was Rehema's plan all along. To keep her a prisoner until the dragons had gained so much power that none could stand in their way. Rehema had believed she held power over the dragons, and they knew it. She held the secret of the starstone and threatened their existence. When they fought each other, they absorbed the life of the loser. Existing as two and finally becoming one. Now, with Rehema gone, Zabella was all that stood in their way. Did they fear her as they did Rehema? Probably not. Rehema was ruthless, diabolical, even as mad as the dragons. Zabella wondered if she had wasted all that time and now would be the last queen of the maidens.

Her crowning was a somber affair. The maidens sang their songs but with no joy in their hearts. They believed in Zabella. They had faith in her. They just didn't have hope. She didn't need telepathy to know this, she also had lost hope in the world. As the new Queen, she gave her sisters one order, "Go forth and find a champion. Search every corner of this earth and return with a man or woman who is true of heart, a spirit strong as steel, and courage that will shine bright in the darkness."

The war brought out much valor. Heroes, both in uniform and civilian clothes. The miles of trenches were full of heroes who gave their lives to protect the hero next to him. Offering their precious air as the clouds of deadly gas rolled over them. In the cities and towns, men, women, even children carried out deeds that proved they had a heart that beat pure gold. Those hearts were silenced by bullets. Destroyed as shells exploded and turned dugouts and houses into craters. Heroes were easy to find, just not alive.

The dragons' grip was so strong every good and decent person on earth seemed to be swept away. Zabella sat on her throne watching in the pools as her sisters dodged bullets, choked on gas, or perished in the fires of explosions. Only Abagail remained by her side to give her strength and comfort. "Fear not ,sister, we have known war all our lives. This one shall pass too."

"Yes, it will. But when it does will anyone, or anything be left. Can anyone recover from so much hatred. I think not."

"Zabella, you have been looking at this war with eyes of old, or perhaps, not old enough."

'What do you mean, sister?"

"We have been looking for the dragons on different sides of this conflict. As if they are waging war against each other. In the past, they fought for dominance, each dragon trying to outdo or kill another. But they had spent centuries planning their return, they obviously came back with a new vision for this world. Or one that is millennia old. When there were fewer dragons they built empires, I think now they are united in building one great empire to rule over the world.

"They have created an army with artillery that can strike miles away. Underwater boats to sink navies from the darkness of the sea. They even have given man flight in dirigibles and the biplanes to set fires to cities from above. All with one purpose in mind. Where we see two sides locked in combat, they see one great unending war."

The German navy could not defeat the British Grand Fleet on the sea. They resorted to attacking the Allies' shipping lanes, trying to cut off their supplies. The U-boats used a terrifying weapon, the torpedoes, to attack ships while remaining hidden below the waves. They increased their horrific effect by launching them at night. The merchant vessels exploded without warning even while being protected by battleships in a convoy. Their zeppelins were just as effective dropping incendiary bombs on the cities of Britain. Their escort airplanes kept the Allies' fighters busy as the large airships darkened the skies and set fire to the cities below.

A throwback to the chivalries of the knights, pilots engaged in dogfights, as a one-on-one battle for personal honor. The pilots fell to earth in defeat, never to soar again. The antiaircraft guns were able to turn back the air fleet but not before great demoralizing damage could be inflicted on the population. "Together, these forces have made this war the greatest ever fought, but it also means no winner to take control of man's world. It seems to me, they are acting on a singular intention. You have touched their world through Rehema, have you not found one undeniable force directing this war?"

"I have felt many minds pushing for this world, but you may be right. They all seem to have one driving force. The Central Powers controlled by a consortium of dragons make sense to me. It also means that the dragons are probably ruling them from a single location. Their powers would be more effective if they learned to use it together as we do. They must have learned the technique from Rehema while they were still in their ruby cradles. Practiced and honed their abilities before their release into a world primed by Rehema and ready for domination. I feel this power is centered in the Wetterstein Mountains. I would say Zugspitze is their home."

"We only need to find one person to lead them out of the darkness. Mankind has a great capacity to heal, to mend hearts and minds. Their greatest asset is they can forget and move on. We will find the one who will show them the way forward." Abigail's eyes glowed with hope and strength. She had been in the world as it turned into the turmoil of one war after another. Each time, she had felt mankind had taken a step closer to greatness. But she was disappointed that it could not free itself. They always slid down into another conflict.

"Do you truly believe there is such a person left on this earth?"

"As iron is turned to steel, and carbon crushed into diamond, the greater the despair the more powerful the champion. We must not give up the search. You have a weapon that will bring the dragons to their end. You will find the right person to wield it."

"You are right, Abagail! I must find this person. It is up to me to search for our champion. It is my light that will draw him. I need to be out there. I am the beacon of hope."

ABOUT THE AUTHOR

About The Author

James L Hill, a.k.a. J L Hill, is a multi-genre author, currently working on a three-part historical fantasy; The Gemstone Series, comprising of *The Emerald Lady*—which has been published. *The Ruby Cradle*, due out soon, and the third book, *The Diamond Warrior*, in the near future.

The *four-part adult urban crime series, The Killer Series,* is completed. *Killer With A Heart, Killer With Three Heads*, *Killer With Black Blood,* and *Killer With Ice Eyes* have all received great reviews. The last two novels were runners-up in the Killer Nashville's contests of 2022.

Then there is the psychological dystopian science fiction thriller, *Pegasus: A Journey To New Eden* for your reading pleasure.

Horror will be the next genre covered. *The House of Sun and Shadow* will be tackled in the coming months.

ALSO BY JAMES L HILL

Adult Crime Fiction

The Killer Series

Book 1: Killer with a Heart

Book 2: Killer with Three Heads

Book 3: Killer with Black Blood

Book 4: Killer with Ice Eyes

Science Fiction

Pegasus: A Journey to New Eden

Fantasy

The Gemstone Series

Book 1: The Emerald Lady

EXCERPT

The Gemstone Series

Book 1
 The Emerald Lady

Chapter 1
Shipwreck

Jack Roggies was a twelve-year-old ship's boy. Young for the position, being two to four years prior to the normal, but he was hard working even if lacking the strength needed to haul water to the men on deck. Nevertheless, he was spry and agile as someone his age should be, able to avoid getting in the way of the men working the lines and sheets. Also, quick to respond to anyone's call, and not just Captain Meyers or Midshipman Simmons, he had earned his nickname, Jack Quick, by being the fastest to reach the Fore Royal Mast, and was best suited for the job of ship's lookout.

Jack was in awe of the enormous size of the Rummy Gale, the biggest ship in Portsmouth, and had to learn all the stores quickly, going up and down the four lower decks, running the 220-feet bow to aft and being reminded constantly, in his first week at sea, that all things must be done on the double.

The Rummy Gale was a Dutch-built Indiaman, large and heavy, made for hauling cargo. She had seen better days at sea but she was still steady in her timbers, and had recently gone through a careening for a thorough cleaning and tarring. She was a solid 1,422-ton beast of the sea empty but on this voyage, she was hauling two hundred tons of lumber. As a result, she was riding a little low, as noted by the Captain.

Jack called down from his perch 187-feet above the deck, "dark clouds on the horizon dead ahead. I see God's anger."

"Give a heading to steer clear," called the Midshipman.

"No clearing, Mr. Simmons, solid wall from end to end. Lots of heaven's fire too."

"Come down, boy. A storm can be upon us quicker than even you can climb," yelled the Captain.

"Aye, aye, Captain." Jack started down the shroud. Descending to the foremast, he spotted something off starboard, and hooking his arm through the ropes, he pulled the spyglass from his trousers, scanned the waves alongside the ship, and noticed a bloody red body appear and sink below the waves. He yelled, "man overboard, off starboard!"

Jeremy Simmons raced to the gunwale, several sailors taking up position along the side also, all searching for a man in the water.

The Captain called up. "Give a bearing, boy!"

Jack pointed towards the bow, "it was there, Sir! A league distance, streaked with blood and tossed in the waves."

The Captain scanned from where the boy pointed backwards. "Do any of you men see it, or any debris in the water?"

A chorus of, "nay," rumbled down the length of the ship.

The Captain looked across the horizon through his spyglass and ordered the boy back up the shroud to his perch with instructions to be on watch for a ship's mast. Then he called Jeremy Simmons over. "Don't keep him aloft too long, and keep a lookout for any sign of a shipwreck on the horizon."

"What's your thinking, Captain?"

"I'm thinking that a boy his age should not be on my ship, Mr. Simmons. It is a fine age for the navy, who can afford to train a boy to be an officer and a gentleman. But this is a commercial ship, I cannot afford to pay a boy who can't earn his keep."

"Yes, Sir. But as I explained before we embarked, his father died and he is the eldest of his mother's sons. He needs to earn a crossing wage, if the family is to survive, so he will be my responsibility." Then wanting to veer the conversation in another direction, Jeremy asked. "What about the body in the water?"

"I saw no body," stated Captain Meyers, "what's more, I see no wreckage that would accompany a body this far out. Did you?"

"No, Sir." Jeremy agreed.

"My thinking is; this is the first of many storms we will encounter on this passage, and a boy just from his mother's teat is full of fear of what a storm at sea brings. As right he should be. If he does not spot a mast hiding among the clouds, or any wreckage in the waves soon, send him below to ride out the storm."

The Captain knew that a body in the water, unaccompanied by any other sign of wreckage, was a known pirate's trick to get a ship to luff and becalm her sails. Then they would come racing out of the coverage of the storm and take the ship while it was busy rescuing a person long-time dead. Likewise, the absence of another ship could be a sign of something even more dangerous to come.

As the bank of black clouds appeared before the Rummy Gale, Jeremy Simmons ordered Jack Quick from the riggings, and replaced him with other sailors reefing the upper sails in preparation for the storm. Thunder rolled across the waves and Jack shuddered as he, and Jeremy made their way to the Captain's quarters.

Jeremy, towering over the frail boy, placed a firm hand on his shoulder, "a storm is a storm, the same at sea as on land. It is just a bit of wind, water, and wailing. Calm yourself, Jack."

"Yes Sir."

"Oh, but it is not just a storm when you are at sea." The Captain contradicted the midshipman, as he stood in the cabin's doorway watching the men prepare. The waves already rocking the ship even as heavy as she was.

The storm was still several hours ahead, but Jack was right, it stretched from port to starboard with not a break in sight and he hoped the wall of black did not go on for too long. Jeremy had convinced him that carrying milled lumber would increase the load and therefore the profit of the voyage, but it also meant that the ship was much heavier, ride lower in the waves, and be more prone to sinking in a violent storm. "On land, a storm does not open the ground beneath your feet and pull you under. Now, what did you see from your lookout, Master Roggies?"

"You mean the body," Jack said carefully, as he was quite afraid of the Captain. The grey beard was rugged and unkempt, and the face hard and scarred. "I saw a body with long streaks of blood down its back. But the blood was bright crimson, like fire, it was there for but a moment, then gone."

The Captain led them into his cabin and poured the young boy a full glass of grog. Four times his daily ration. Then he lit up his pipe, taking several strong pulls to get it going. Smoke whorls streamed from his nose and surrounded his weathered face. "Ah, you saw your first mermaid, my boy."

"Captain!" Jeremy objected. "Do you think it wise to fill the boy's head with fancies?"

The Captain laughed. "Fancies, Mr. Simmons? You went to sea as a lad a little older than good ol' Jack Quick here, been on the water some six years now, and you think you have seen all there is. I walked a deck since the day I could walk at my father's side, I have seen monsters. Fish the size of a ship that can reduce this boat to driftwood. They surface without warning and send clouds into the skies. And yes, mermaids too. They either come to lead us through a storm safely, or to collect our souls for the devil."

"As to your giant fish, I have heard of them, although I have never seen one myself," Jeremy said, lighting up his pipe, the red glow reflecting the copper streaks in his hair, which was tied tight into a neat ponytail and his equally freshly minted copper eyes lit up brighter as he spoke passionately. "But I have never heard one creditable story of a mermaid. Most are told by those who have had as many years of grog as actual sea duty, and are usually told in exchange for a pint." He laughed. "And they all end with the rum-soaked brain being unable to forget her face, or the love gained and lost in a single glance."

Jack's eyes widened as saucers and glossed over as another wave rocked the Rummy Gale.

The captain squared him up, "a man might well take rum as his mistress once his heart has been touched by a mermaid. Drown himself in drink, as it were, to finish the job left undone by the sea. Jack, my boy, you be too young to feel this now, but I assure thee there be no purer love for a sailor than that for the maidens of the sea."

"You said they come for our souls."

"Well, not all love is reciprocated," claimed the captain.

The boy became unsteady on his feet again, and Jeremy, several inches taller than the Captain was at six-feet caught his arm and steadied him before letting go. "Finish your grog, Jack, then, go below and help me secure our load."